1

GARDEN CENTER

I t was a still, Sunday morning, save for a sparrow. The panicked bird fitfully flapped its wings, tip-tapping its beak against a cloudy window from inside the small garden center as it tried to escape. The bird's spastic attempt at freedom distracted Rochelle Hawthorne.

Poor bird. Rochelle forced herself to concentrate so she wouldn't forget the list of items she'd memorized. Items, usually neatly written on a monogrammed pad, were now jumbled in her head as they tried to disappear. Rochelle lived by lists. She wrote them down, and rewrote them once again, tidy and organized. She'd even put the items in order of location inside the store, to make for a more efficient trip—but not today. Today, she didn't dare make a list of the items she needed. Today, she was going to have to remember.

Towels. The bird appeared to be exhausting itself trying to escape. *There's an open door right below the window. You flew in through that same door!*

Rochelle had problems of her own. She wrestled with a creaking metal shopping cart, as she jockeyed it through unkempt aisles, resenting its errant front wheel. It was hard enough keeping her thoughts in line...*towels*...never mind trying to steer an erratic buggy with a wandering front end. On top of that, she could still hear the desperate bird in the background. *Flutter-flutter, tip-tap.* Rochelle grabbed a small stack of white terry towels and placed them in the cart.

Lye. A regular at her local garden center, everyone there knew Rochelle by her first name. Which was why she chose this particular store, secluded in the country, many towns away from her own. No one would know her here. *There it is!* Lifting the plastic bag of lye from the shelf, she read the words *caustic* and *food grade* and wondered how a thing could possibly be both. She placed the package of lye into the cart. *Uhm...shovel.*

The malodorous scent of mulch hung in the air as Rochelle forced her cart to make the turn at the end of one aisle into the next, causing its stubborn wheel to lock and sprag along the floor, leaving a black skid mark on the concrete. *Flutter-flutter, tip-tap.* She spied the shovels and made her way toward them. She eyed the jumbled lot, their handles leaning against each other like drunken cowboys.

She pulled a pointed shovel from the dented and dusty rack, lifting her sunglasses to get a better look at the shovel's sharp tip. *This should cut easily through the wretched Texas clay soil.*

"Well, that's a beaut!" The voice behind her startled Rochelle.

"Excuse me?" she turned and asked the old man—Earl, according to the name tag pinned to his orange vest. Aside from his vest, he was very beige: beige khakis, beige work boots, a plaid flannel shirt with varying shades of beige. Even his white hair, tinged by nicotine, was indicative of a middle school lunch tray.

"That shovel there! It's quite a beauty! That tip'll slice through anythin'. You buyin' that for yer husband, little darlin'?"

Yes. "No, it's for me," she forced a horizontal smile. *Oh no, what else did I need?*

"For you? I wouldn't be expectin' a fancy lady like you to be gettin' all dirty." Earl laughed until he wheezed.

"I love to garden...is it Earl?"

"Yessiree, ma'am. Earl McCreedy! I been workin' this garden center for sixty years. Haven't seen ya in these parts before."

Rochelle slowly tightened her grip on the shovel, stretching her knuckles ever so slightly. "I'm sorry, what did you say? I'm in a bit of a hurry."

"Haven't seen ya in the store before. What kinda gardenin' do you do? Vegetable or flower?"

"Uhm...flower." Rochelle was desperate to be on her way, but there was one more thing she needed...if only she could remember. *Flutter-flutter, tip-tap.*

"Yeah, I figured. I saw that-there lye in yer cart. Hydrangeas?"

"Hydrangeas?" Rochelle bit her lip. "No, I don't need any hydrangeas, thanks."

Earl laughed until he coughed, then wheezed—long and constricted, the kind one earns from sucking on two packs a day since childhood. Rochelle visualized his gray lungs clamping in fear, not wanting to allow in another putrid and poisonous smoke-filled breath. *What was it I needed?* She thought hard while Earl regained his composure.

"You sure are funny lil missy. I was just thinkin' that maybe yer buyin' that lye to change the color of yer hydrangeas 'cause lye'll turn 'em from blue to pink if you amend the soil just right."

"Uh...em, yeah," she lied, "that's what I'm using it for." *Now can I get the hell out of here? Flutter-flutter, tip-tap.*

"Thing is...I see yer buyin' that-there shovel, with that-there cuttin' edge. Makes me get to thinkin' you got that real stubborn clay soil. You know...the kind that when ya stomp that new shovel in there reeaal good...you hear that suction...that clay stickin' to the metal like a guppy? And ya pull that clump of earth out and it's huggin' the blade, and then ya have to clean the head of the shovel every time? Before ya stick it back in the ground?"

Rochelle's head was spinning, white knuckles clamped to the shovel's shaft. *Shut up, shut up! There's something I've GOT to remember! Flutter-flutter, tip-tap.*

"Well...that stubborn clay soil is alkaline as can be, so ya won't be needin' that lye to make yer hydrangeas pink." Earl's eyes, magnified and distorted by his coke-bottle lenses, squinted at Rochelle, then cut to her cart. "What else ya got in there?"

Rochelle quickly placed the shovel in the cart, its handle stuck out and forward like a knight's lance, ready to strike its opponent, and headed for the register, away from Earl and his questions.

"Have yerself a blessed day, young lady!" Earl called out, as Rochelle forced her rebellious buggy across the floor. "Y'all come back again, ya hear?"

Think, think, THINK! Keep moving forward. Earl's hacking receded in the distance as Rochelle made her way toward the front of the store, and the unsuccessful bird. *Just four inches lower.*

"Hey," the cashier droned, "welcome to McCreedy's General…" Rochelle felt the eyes of the raven-haired teen scan her from top to bottom while fiddling with what seemed to be a fresh eyebrow piercing. The girl's black T-shirt, emblazoned with a faded UFO and the words *I Want To Believe,* appeared to be cut apart and then reassembled with hundreds of safety pins. "Are you a celebrity or somethin'?"

"No," replied Rochelle, wishing there was a self-checkout kiosk in the antiquated store. "Why do you ask?" Rochelle watched white teeth and a bubblegum tongue, stark against matte black lips, as the girl answered.

"Well…you got those big shades on, and that mole on your cheek, well, you kinda look like Marilyn Monroe except you're skinny and got red hair."

"Oh, ha." Rochelle regretted not pulling her long red hair into a ponytail and hiding it under a baseball cap. She removed the supplies from her cart and placed them on the counter. *Flutter-flutter, tip-tap.* The checkout girl appeared unfazed by the bird.

"I'm gonna be a celebrity one day…"

Rochelle wasn't paying attention to the girl pressing buttons on the register. Her mind wandered through its checklist as she watched items disappear into a brown paper bag.

Beep. Rope…to bind the hands and feet. Beep. Plastic…to wrap the body. Beep. Duct tape…to seal the plastic. Beep. Beep. Towels and bleach…to clean up the mess. Beep. Lye…to dissolve the body. Beep…Beep…Beeee…

"Ma'am. Ma'am, MA'AM!" Rochelle was snapped out of her

daydream by the cashier, infected brow furrowed. "Will you be needing anything else?"

I need someone to help the damn bird! "Uhm, no... YES! Gloves!" Rochelle remembered and grabbed a pair of rubberized gardening gloves from the small rack next to the cash register and placed them on the counter. *Can't leave fingerprints.*

"That'll be ninety-one eighty-six." The girl chewed at what was left of her black nail polish as Rochelle swiped her credit card. *Flutter-flutter, tip-tap.* "Be careful with that lye, it's pretty caustic. You can get some real bad burns if it touches your skin for too long. EARL...CARRY OUT!" The cashier ripped the receipt from the register. "Did you know you can actually dissolve a human body if you mix that stuff with wa—?"

Rochelle was already out the door, fast-walking to her car, hugging the paper shopping bag. *Stupid bird!* She opened her car door, threw the bag over onto the passenger seat, and hopped in, not bothering to buckle the belt as she skidded out of the store's parking lot onto the gravel road. In her rearview mirror, through a cloud of dust, she saw Earl, standing in the parking lot, Rochelle's forgotten shovel in hand, raised in the air, as if to summon her back. There was no turning back.

Rochelle was good at gardening. She was good at everything. She wondered if she would also be good at disposing of her husband's dead body.

2

BROKEN CHINA

Two days before...
Fourteen!

Harrison Henry Hawthorne III ducked, eluding heirloom porcelain as it whizzed by his head, exploding into the wall behind him. *CRASH!*

"What the fuck, Rochelle?"

Thirteen!

Another of the priceless plates, handed down through four generations of the Hawthorne family, flew by—this time nicking his ear. *CRASH!*

Twelve.

"JESUS CHRIST! STOP! Have you lost your goddamned mind?" Harry yelled at his wife through his hands as he shielded his face from what he feared to be the next impending projectile.

Rochelle stood in position, barefoot in her dining room, a fragile warrior armed with plate in hand, ready to hurl another eight-hundred-dollar disc at her husband, but didn't dare. Not because the piece was expensive and irreplaceable. Not because she knew this time she would hit him square between the eyes. But, simply because there was no way she was going to settle for less than twelve perfect dinner plates in her china cabinet. Service for twelve was the magic number. Anything less was unacceptable.

"ARRGH, Harry!" Rochelle's wild red hair haloed around her, accentuating her frustration. "Tonight's dinner means a lot to me!"

"I know, babe." Rochelle didn't believe him. Harry slowly raised his hands in surrender. "But I've *got* to be at the office, the VC's are arriving today. The meeting shouldn't go past 6:00."

"You own the company, Harry. You know you could've scheduled the meeting for yesterday—for any other day, just not today!" Rochelle forced herself to release her grip on the priceless plate and placed it onto one of the silver chargers on the meticulously decorated dining room table. *Twelve.*

Harry exhaled. "It'll be great! You always host phenomenal events." His attempt at a compliment only made it worse.

Rochelle clenched her fists and pulled in a long, deep breath, trying to calm her racing adrenaline. Her perfectly manicured nails made pink marks in her palms. She felt no shame about her tantrum. This was no ordinary dinner Harry was going to be late for. Today was her birthday, and that wasn't the worst of it. Harry forgot.

There was no surprise breakfast in bed, or last minute corny card from the drugstore. There were no presents tied with pretty bows, or generic bouquets of flowers bought at the last harried minute. There was nothing. Just an absentminded husband who had been too busy to notice. Rochelle had been married long enough to Harry to know he put his job before all else, but forget her birthday? Extra hours were no excuse. In an age of smartphones, smartwatches, smart...everything, it was just dumb to forget your wife's birthday.

On top of that, in a matter of hours Rochelle would be hosting her own party, and her husband had no clue. What was going on in his head? It wasn't normal for a wife to hurl dinner plates at her husband, but Harry didn't even think to ask why she was so upset. Rochelle didn't want to be hosting her own party. She wanted to be celebrating with her husband—be celebrated *by* her husband. He could have booked a trip, could have told her he'd made plans for just the two of them for an intimate dinner, could have uttered the words *happy birthday*. But he didn't. Harry had no clue and she was pissed.

"The world will not stop revolving if you take one day off, Harry!" Rochelle continued attempting a slow exhale as she wrapped her arms around her own thin frame.

"I know Ro, but..."

Rochelle's thoughts trailed off...going to that place again...they *always* went to that place. She wished she'd had children. Maybe she wouldn't be so lonely. Maybe she wouldn't pressure Harry, or care so much that he was a workaholic who had no time to remember her one special day. If she'd been able to have children, she'd have someone in her life to take care of, someone who would love her back—the right way.

They tried to have children, but she couldn't hold a baby in her broken womb, and Harry didn't like the thought of adoption. So it was just the two of them—and Moosh, her Bichon. She doted on that dog like she would a child. He was her baby, she loved him with all her heart, and he, in turn, showed her the unconditional love she so desired.

Maybe she was silly to wish for what she didn't have. Maybe she should be grateful she had what she did. Rochelle was talented —gifted, blessed with a creative eye for detail. It was her discerning eye and green thumb that created the spectacular gardens on their property. Lush beds of flowers and shrubs encompassed the soft green yard. She also had a knack for throwing a grand affair, hosting lavish dinner parties for her intimate group of friends. Rochelle was known to wow with her dinner parties—perfection at every turn, each table-scape better than the next. She enjoyed doing it, loved creating an experience for an eclectic gathering of friends at her table. She felt it nourished not only body and soul, but the imagination as well. There was nothing better than sharing good food and good conversation in an inspired setting.

She loved it all, except for today. On any other day, a small party of six would be no big deal, but today was different. Today, resentment reigned. Forget her workaholic husband. Why couldn't her friends take on the responsibility of planning for *her?* She knew why. It was clear when Maeve called her two weeks ago to break the news.

$$\sim$$

"Sweetie, it's not that we want y'all to do all the work," Maeve Spencer reassured her best friend. "It's just that…well, there is no way on God's green earth any one of us nitwits can create as beautiful an atmosphere as you, honey."

"But it doesn't matter to me how any of you do it. What matters to me is *that* you do it."

"Awww Roey, you know you not only host fabulous shindigs, but you create an experience beyond anyone's wildest dreams."

"Anyone can do that, Maeve."

"You're too modest, honeybee. No one can do it like you, and we're all afraid, if we host, you'll be lookin' at every little detail and judgin' it by your standards. None of us are gonna live up to that."

"I am not going to judge anyone!"

"Oh yes you will! You'll be gettin' out that mini measurin' tape you hide in your Chanel bag and you'll be calculatin' how far the silverware is from the plate."

Rochelle chuckled, she loved Maeve. "I will not! Who measures flatware?"

"You see? Flatware! I don't even know what the dang words are!"

"Don't play dumb with me, Maeve. We both know how smart you are."

Rochelle was right about that. Maeve was five foot eight, blonde, voluptuous, and smart as a whip. Despite being raised in a trailer in the South, in a situation without much promise, she was smarter and better read than anyone Rochelle knew…regardless of dropping her g's. Those who didn't know Maeve were quick to stereotype her as a vapid blonde on looks alone, but they'd be wrong. Most importantly, she was a good friend to Rochelle. She was loyal and honest and down to earth, despite being married to a billionaire.

"So, whaddya say, honeybee? You up to creatin' a beautiful evenin'? We'll bring the booze and apps if you want."

Rochelle smiled to herself, proud of her friend, who's life was now charmed. For as fate would have it, after putting herself through college working multiple jobs, she would meet her husband, Barrington Avery Spencer, twenty-six years her senior, working an internship in the accounting department of his tech company. Rochelle loved that Maeve still kept her humble heart.

"OK Maeve, it's no problem. And don't worry about the drinks and apps, I'll figure it out." If Rochelle was going to host an event, then she was going to do it all herself.

"Great! Kisses!"

ROCHELLE FIGURED she could at least count on Harry to stay home and help her, but now he was making excuses. "Come on, babe." Harry wrapped his arms around Rochelle and squeezed. She didn't return the hug. Her arms stayed clamped to her middle as she peered around her husband, eyeing the table-scape she just spent the past two weeks planning. "I promise I'll be back as early as possible."

"Don't make promises you can't keep, Harry."

"You have my word, Ro. Besides, I've got to drop off some medical paperwork to HR for the new insurance."

"Then you'd better grab the file from my desk."

"Already did."

"And you couldn't have done *that* yesterday?"

"I forgot."

"That's the problem, Harry, you always forget. Everything!" She pushed him away. "You're so laser focused on work, you neglect everything else in your life until *you* are ready to spend the time. Then you expect everyone else to drop what they're doing. You need to get it together, Harry! Learn how to balance."

"Yeah, I'll learn balance when you learn how to set a table." With that, Harry childishly tugged on the embroidered white silk tablecloth, discombobulating Rochelle's perfect place settings. Harry then scurried out of the house and hopped into his car, evading the rest of the conversation.

"Harrison Hawthorne!" Rochelle ran after her husband, the man-child, and yelled from the front door, "I'll kill you!"

Rochelle didn't see the startled paperboy run off as she turned to go back inside. She was frustrated with her husband, his forgetfulness, and his childish ways, but she forced herself to bury that deep, in order to continue prepping for the evening's festivities. Harry's little prank would set her back at least an hour, she still had to pick up Moosh from the groomer, and on top of that, there was broken china to sweep.

She couldn't believe she'd thrown those plates. So many times, she thought of doing something like that, but never dared. She kind of liked the way it felt—being out of control, it was powerful.

Removing a broom and dustpan from her mudroom, Rochelle noticed Harry's forgotten work satchel on the kitchen counter, half-opened and brimming with files and paperwork. *Typical Harry.* Surely he would be calling any minute to ask her to run it to his car. She knew the drill.

Rochelle placed the broom and dustpan aside, picked up the briefcase, and headed toward the front door. Not paying attention to where she was stepping, her bare foot found an errant piece of broken porcelain. The sharp shard stung as it pierced her skin, causing her to drop Harry's satchel to the ground as she grabbed her foot, splaying all of the satchel's contents on the slick marble tiles. *Dammit!*

Irritated with herself for being so careless, she sat on the cold floor and huffed. She squeezed the skin on the underside of her foot with her champagne colored manicured nails and removed the tiny embedded shard. A red pinprick of blood blossomed through her pale skin, quelling her short-lived rebelliousness. Rochelle felt embarrassed by her outburst and the mess she made. Her face felt flush thinking of how childishly she'd behaved. Guilt set in. Harry was a good provider, she shouldn't make him feel bad for working hard to support them both. She'd apologize later.

On her hands and knees, Rochelle carefully gathered the array of doctor's receipts and medical records. Pushing them together, she stuffed the papers back into the file folder. It bothered her, not arranging the paperwork by date, but she had too much work to do. She opened Harry's bag—it smelled of old leather and airplanes—and rolled her eyes at the ink-stained bottom. She reached inside to remove a broken pen and a few lint-covered breath mints, escaped from their tin. *Does he even know what's in here?*

Rochelle tugged a loose thread inside the bag, it didn't come readily, instead, it caused the thin suede lining to buckle. She wondered how Harry could stand his bag in such disarray as she attempted to smooth the lining down with her hand as best she could. It resisted her efforts. There was something underneath. Opening the bag wider for a better view, she lifted the loose corner of the lining, revealing the edge of a pink paper. She pinched the tightly folded paper and slid it out. Was it purposely hidden inside the lining? She unfolded the paper and smoothed it out to read the fading print from a doctor she didn't recognize.

Rochelle was confused, as she normally made all the medical appointments. Harry wasn't that responsible, or interested. Familiar with Harry's doctors, every name was programmed into Rochelle's phone. She knew every receptionist, and had every important receipt in that file, in order by date of service—until today. The additional pink paper with fading text, tucked into the lining, appeared to be from eight years ago, only two years into their young marriage.

Harry had seen a Dr. Moneesh Aziz at Presbyterian General. There was no service listed, just a code *CPT-55250*. Rochelle kept that paper for herself.

3

MAEVE AND BARRINGTON

"My tits still look good, don't they?" A naked Maeve Spencer stood in front of the gilt framed mirror in her massive master bathroom staring at herself.

"Your tits look great for thirty-nine." Maeve's husband came up from behind and wrapped his arms around her, grabbing her oversized breasts. They both stared at her reflection. "And when they don't, we'll buy you new ones."

"I don't know if I'll want new ones, baby. I think I'm gonna just grow old gracefully."

"Forget that!" Barrington said, releasing his embrace and playfully slapping her bare ass. "No wife of mine is going to look old."

"Are you kiddin' me?" Maeve removed her white shirred dress from the padded valet hanger and stepped into it. "I didn't say I wanted to LOOK old." She shimmied to pull the tight dress up and over her hourglass curves and perfect breasts. "There's a difference between growin' old gracefully and lookin' old. I'm gonna grow old gracefully. I've decided. Can you zip me?"

Barrington Avery Spencer III zipped his wife's dress. "Very well then, when that happens, I'll be trading you in for a newer model."

She knew he wasn't lying.

"Aw baby, you'll be dead before I allow that to happen."

They both knew *she* wasn't lying. Maeve rose on bare tiptoes to kiss her husband, leaving a red lipstick print on his mouth. The southern bombshell was five foot nine but still had to reach for a kiss, as Barrington towered over her at six foot five. Maeve slipped into her heels as she watched him fumble with his bow tie.

"Here, baby, lemme help you with that." Barrington turned to face her. Maeve was happy to have his full attention as she easily crossed, folded, and pulled the silk into a perfect bow, a task she'd done so many times before. "Now remember, tonight is Rochelle's birthday, so try not to be an ass."

"What do you mean by that?"

"You know what I mean, you and the boys and Mirabelle get to talkin' business, then politics, and then all holy hell breaks loose. All that posturin' to see who can be the prettier peacock when all y'all really look like y'all don't know split beans from coffee."

"Pumpkin, I don't know what you're talking about."

"You certainly do!" Maeve patted her husband's chest. "There, how's that?"

Barrington checked his tie in the mirror, as well as his own reflection. "Perfect." At sixty-five he looked quite young save for his white hair. "Why is Rochelle hosting her own birthday, anyway?" He poured himself a scotch from the crystal decanter set on the elaborate rolling bar cart in their master bath.

"Because none of us can throw a party the way that girl can! She's got a gift from God the way she can create an atmosphere. It'd just be a letdown for her, if one of us hosted. But we'll certainly lift her up tonight and celebrate her properly."

"Why didn't that dolt Harry rent out the Ritz or something? He's got the money. Why should she have to slave on her own birthday?"

"I don't know, baby. Maybe he's got a lot goin' on at work."

"Then he should have hired someone—what a fool."

"OK now, see, there ya go."

Barrington grabbed his wife by the waist and pulled her close. "All I know, pumpkin, if it were *your* birthday, I would spare no expense. I would fly you to Paris and have Cartier open the store just for you. I would hire Bobby Flay to bake your birthday cake. I would pamper you the way you deserve to be pampered."

Maeve giggled at her husband. "Silly chicken, Bobby Flay isn't a baker!" She felt her husband's firmness as he pressed against her.

"Then I'll buy him baking lessons so that he can bake your cake." Barrington unzipped the back of his wife's dress and kissed her neck.

"Mmmm...what kind of cake?" Maeve felt heat wash over her body as her dress slipped to the floor.

"Any kind of cake you want," he answered, sliding one hand up into her hair and the other down the small of her back, pulling her even closer.

Maeve's body tingled as she and her husband kissed. "Bar...we've got to go..." She couldn't resist his warm breath on her neck, on her breasts, on her abdomen, as he slid his hands between her legs. "Mmm...gon...be late..."

"Just five minutes..."

"OK..."

4

MIRABELLE AND CHRISTOPHER

Christopher Campbell dropped speared sour cherries into the rosy drinks he prepared for himself and his best friend, Mirabelle. As he listened, she continue to grill her twin daughters.

"...and what is the capital of Switzerland?"

"Bern." The girls answered in unison.

"What is their currency?"

"Franc." They answered correctly.

"What is the capital of Canada?"

"Ottawa," they harmonized.

"And the currency?"

"Ummmm..."

Mirabelle Huang-Chung, self-proclaimed tiger mom, tapped her Christian Louboutins impatiently on the imported bamboo floor.

"Ummmm..." The twins refused to make eye contact with their stern mother.

"It's the dollar girls—the Canadian dollar!" Mirabelle rolled her eyes in frustration, shaking her head.

"That was a trick question!" Ivy protested.

It was six thirty in the evening, Ivy and her ten-year-old twin, Lily, were still in their summer school uniforms sitting at their kitchen counter as their mother quizzed them.

"It was NOT a trick question and the two of you should be smarter than that! How do you expect to get into Harvard if you don't know the answers to the simplest questions?"

"We're TEN, Mom!" Lily whined.

"Yes, and in the blink of an eye you will be twenty-five and working at Walmart! Go upstairs and take your baths. When you are finished, I want you to read up on Canada, and each of you type a one-thousand-word essay on its history, then practice your violin, then in to bed you go."

"Maahumm!" they whined in unison.

"Grandma's upstairs, let her know when you're finished and she will tuck you in. Say goodnight to Uncle Christopher."

"Goodnight, Uncle Christopherrrr..."

The girls stood side by side, mini unkempt versions of their mother, with almond eyes, rosy lips, and long, black hair that hung in their faces.

"Goodnight, divaasss!" he sang, then with hand to mouth, whispered, "Forget Harvard, twinkies. You can both marry sugar daddies."

"Eewwww!" they screamed as they ran off and up the stairs, giggling all the way, until their voices faded.

"I heard that!" Mirabelle scolded her friend. "Give me that drink!"

Christopher slid the drink across the sage onyx countertop to Mirabelle. "Those two scare me."

"The girls?" she asked.

"Yeah, they look like a Chinese version of *The Shining* twins!"

"Oh my God...you're such a fucking ass." Mirabelle sipped. Her red, one-shoulder dress, made of mulberry silk, was embroidered with a sinuous dragon intertwined with delicate flowers. The design made her appear more like an Asian princess than a suburban mother. "Mmmm, this is great!"

"It's a Cherry Bomb, my love. You really should ease up on those two, let them be kids. How do I look?" he asked, adjusting his bow tie and smoothing his plum brocade jacket.

"You look great. Like a gay James Bond. What do you mean ease up? Am I *that* bad?"

Christopher raised his manicured eyebrows, taking a sip of his drink.

"It's a hard world out there." Mirabelle protested. Her exotic eyes, black diamonds, were laser focused and not backing down.

"In the fifth grade?"

"In the world...you have no idea...I'm going to have to up their tutoring. Kids are competing NOW to get into college. I can't have them slacking. High school SATs are right around the corner. They need to be studying!"

"OMG darling, when I was in high school, the only thing I was studying was Billy Janikowski in his tighty-whities."

"Yeah, well, look where it's gotten you."

"What?" Christopher grabbed his chest and feigned offense. "I'm a VERY successful interior designer. Look around darling, your perfect manse is fabulous because of *moi*!"

Mirabelle sipped her drink. Christopher was right, at least about the impeccable decor in her exquisite home. He was a gifted designer with an eye for detail but wouldn't know the first thing about rearing children, especially Chinese children. No one was going to do that better than Mirabelle. She knew what was expected. She needed to be in control, and the twins were going to be top-notch.

"Why so strict, tiger? You and Chao are multi-millionaires. Those girls are set for life."

"Christopher, you're American, I can't imagine you'd ever understand. It's a different culture. Chinese children are expected to excel. Not just live off of their parents' fortunes."

"But we're not in China, hon. We're in the United States and those girls *do* excel. I mean, they are only ten, and, by my accounts, they are way ahead of kids twice their age."

"Exactly, and it's going to stay that way until they graduate with doctorate degrees. Then they can do whatever the fuck they want."

"Sheesh, I'm all for strong women, Mir, and I can tell you, if you push them too hard they are going to turn into rebellious little bitches...and believe me...I should know...*I* was a rebellious little bitch."

"Chris, you're still a rebellious little bitch."

"Cheers to that!" The two friends clinked glasses. "Anyway, I wouldn't worry about the twinkies, Barrington's kids are idiots, and they got into Harvard."

"True." They both sipped without saying a word.

As Christopher lowered his glass, Mirabelle noticed a glint of something on his left hand. "New ring?"

"Ah, yes, darling."

"Lemme see that."

Christopher held out his hand for his friend to inspect the slim gold band on his ring finger. Two tiny stones, a sapphire and a ruby, sat next to each other, like handsome brothers, embedded deep into the band.

"This is gorgeous, is it an heirloom?"

"Not an heirloom, but a custom piece."

"Where'd you get this?"

Christopher raised his glass to his lips and batted his eyelashes to keep from answering his friend.

"Is this from one of *your* sugar daddies?"

"Yup, from the sweetest of them all."

"Sheesh...I'm keeping you away from my girls from now on. You are a horrible role model! I don't want them catching affluenza!"

Christopher playfully swatted his friend. "You're such an ass."

"Haha! Takes one to know one. What do you say? Let's get going. Don't want to be late for Rochelle's party. Do you have your gift?"

"Yes, it's in the car, and it's fabulous—after you, my dear." Christopher gestured to Mirabelle, who grabbed a golden box wrapped with a beautiful silk scarf intricately tied into a knot. emulating a lotus flower. The two friends headed out the front door to the waiting driver.

5

PINK EDGES

Tiny diamonds assembled into starbursts adorned the vintage French hair comb once belonging to Harry's great-grandmother. Hands trembling ever so slightly, Rochelle carefully nestled the platinum adornment into the pulled-back side of her long, flame waves. A whisper of liquid liner on her upper lids and an extra coat of mascara was all she needed to accentuate her emerald eyes. Vermilion lips and the silver silk dress she'd commissioned for the occasion made her feel like a movie star, complementing the Old Hollywood theme of her birthday dinner.

Harry still wasn't home, and guests would start arriving in half an hour. Rochelle didn't care anymore. She had a change of plans. At the last minute, she called in a favor from a friend and arranged for a small catering service to handle the party. She wasn't going to be distracted by having to do all the work. She had a plan that was going to make for an unforgettable evening.

She reached down for the high heels nestled beside her stool and scratched Moosh's head, coercing him into releasing one of the straps with which he happily played. She slid on her heels, careful not to disturb the Band-Aid on the underside of her punctured right foot. The broken porcelain she stepped on left a small cut, and she didn't want it to stain her new silver Jimmy Choos. She buckled the delicate ankle straps and rose from her stool. Smoothing the front of her dress, which emphasized her willowy frame, she did a half twirl to examine the plunging back décolleté. *Perfect.*

Lifting the silver hand mirror from her dressing table for one more glance, she hoped no one would notice the slightly pink edges rimming her eyes. Pink edges left from the secret tears she'd cried earlier. Pink edges, like the pink paper she found hidden in the lining of Harry's forgotten briefcase. A paper marked with the fading medical code *CPT-55250.* A secret code on a secret paper, from a secret doctor for her forgetful husband's secret vasectomy. The over-the-top tantrum she had earlier was nothing compared to the quiet fury now burning inside.

Rochelle pulled open a drawer in her chiffonier and removed a small, silver box. She opened the box of little peach pills and washed one down with the rest of her martini, tipping her glass to the large mirror in front of her. With glossy eyes and a trembling mouth she whispered, "Happy birthday, babe."

6

ARRIVALS

C andlelight painted the room as tiny beacons of light emanated from cut Waterford crystal. Little fires, glistening atop hand-poured ivory beeswax pillars carefully set within the glass vessels—at least a hundred of them, in varying shapes and sizes—illuminated every inch of the house. The intricate vessels, placed on pedestals, tables, and shelves, tucked in alcoves, and lining the sweeping stairs, created a sea of twinkling light in the dimly lit rooms. Sparkling luminaries, a multitude of stars in a clear night sky.

Rochelle emerged from her bedroom like Hollywood royalty, with a happy Moosh in a tiny bow tie tagging close behind. Her silver silk dress grazed the floor, reflecting the warm candlelight. The diamond comb she'd nestled in her hair as well as the matching brooch attached to the gathered waist of her custom-made dress, created tiny prisms on the walls that glittered and danced in time with the flickering flames.

The bar was set with more crystal, filled with spirits of every kind. The bartender quietly skewered blue cheese–stuffed olives. Rochelle set down her empty martini glass and asked for another. She wasn't feeling the effects of the first one yet.

"Bone dry, please, and I'll be right back."

"Sure thing, Mrs. Hawthorne." The bartender filled a metal

container with ice and vodka, secured the lid, and began to shake it vigorously.

The scintillating scent of rosemary and lamb chops lured Rochelle into her kitchen where the chef and sous chef were busy prepping the meal. She dipped a silver spoon into a simmering pot of gravy and had a small taste of the flavorful creamy concoction, garlic and herbs delighted her palate as Moosh stretched up her leg begging for a turn.

"Wonderful!" She nodded for the chefs to carry on. Moosh yipped for attention. "Smells good, doesn't it, baby? I've got something special just for you." She used the tone of voice people saved for dogs and small children, of which she only had the former. Rochelle headed to the large mud room located at the back of the kitchen, where one of Moosh's crates was housed. Moosh ran up ahead of her in anticipation of his meal. She opened the small refrigerator installed specifically for Moosh's food and took out a small bowl filled with chopped chicken, rice, and peas. She set the bowl in front of her little dog as he tap-danced on the marble tile with anticipatory steps. The dog quickly devoured the delicious meal.

"Settle down little one! You've got to stop inhaling your food. That cannot be good for you." It was too late. The bowl was licked clean, and Moosh was lapping up the water in the other. Rochelle scooped up her little dog when he was finished and opened the door to his wooden crate. She kissed the top of his curly white head and settled him onto a fluffy velvet cushion. "Mommy will be back in a little bit to check on you." As if on cue, the content pup, belly full, curled up to take a nap.

Back at the bar, tiny ice crystals floated atop Rochelle's freshly shaken martini.

"Looks perfect." Rochelle took a sip of the chilled liquid and closed her eyes as she swallowed. How could something be so cold, yet warm her at the same time? It reminded her of Harry. She took a deep breath and tried to forget the pink paper. She could feel tears begin to well behind her lids. *Don't!*

"Yoo-hoo! Is anyone here?" Maeve's voice called out from the foyer.

Rochelle's eyes snapped open and she gulped the rest of her drink, placing the empty glass on the bar.

"Would you like another, Mrs. Haw—"

Rochelle raised a finger to her lips and winked at the bartender. "Shhh...I'm not drinking this evening."

"OH MY GOD, honeybee, you look ah-mazing!" Maeve squealed, enveloping Rochelle in a warm hug.

Rochelle clung to her friend, inhaling Maeve's sweet musk, as she fought back tears. If only Maeve knew how much Rochelle needed that hug.

"So do you, beautiful." Rochelle held her friend's hand high as Maeve spun around in a slow circle. "Good golly, Maeve, if I had that body..."

"You can...for an exorbitant fee," Barrington chimed in as he entered, trying to slap his wife's ass with one hand while juggling a small wrapped gift and a bottle of amber liquid in the other.

"Hand me that present, before you break somethin'." Maeve shooed her husband's hand away while reaching for the delicate box.

Barrington handed the gift to his wife while addressing Rochelle. "Rochelle...happy birthday! Bring it in." He leaned in to give Rochelle a hug, the cloying smell of Scotch whiskey hung heavy on his breath.

A quick pat and Rochelle let go. *Who slaps their wife's ass in public, in this day and age? It's so demeaning.* "Thanks."

"Where's the old man? There's a whiskey that's been waiting a hundred years to break out of this bottle, and tonight's the night we set her free!"

"He should be here any minute." Rochelle actually had no idea when the unreliable liar would be home.

"Where's the bar, then?"

"In there."

Rochelle watched as Barrington headed in toward the unsuspecting bartender, calling out, "My good man..." She was suddenly thankful she hired help. It was like hiring another set of ears to take the brunt of Barrington's narcissistic stories.

"This is for you, sweetie." Maeve handed her friend the little box, wrapped in pink and white gingham paper and delicately bound with a matching pink grosgrain ribbon.

"Aww, you didn't have to." Rochelle's slender fingers fiddled with the bow.

"Of course we did, it's your birthday."

"I'm glad someone remembered." The pink bow reminded her of Harry's secret pink paper.

"You OK, honeybee?"

The concern in her dear friend's eyes touched Rochelle. *I'm falling apart Maeve.* "I'm fine." Rochelle's head felt airy. *Maybe I shouldn't have taken the pill.*

"You sure you're ok? I know you well."

"Yes, it's just that…"

"Bonjours, mes amies!" Christopher sang as he entered the room carrying a gigantic and opulent floral arrangement. Hidden behind the greenery, his eyes, shining slivers of malachite, framed by thick red-rimmed glasses, looked like abstract art as he peeked through the floral stems of the ostentatious monstrosity. "Wow! I'm looking for my friends but all I see are silver screen goddesses!" He and Maeve exchanged two air kisses and then he turned to Rochelle, "Happy birth-day, honey."

"Thank you!" Rochelle's eyes didn't know where to land as she scanned the grandiose arrangement. Long-stemmed white roses and frilly edged tulips were clustered together with exquisite white lilies, hearty ranunculus and fluffy layered peonies. Fresh olive branches topped with white feather butterflies accented the whole thing. The gathering of stems was nestled into a stunning French Lalique Bacchantes vase. "Oh my God, Christopher, this vase is gorgeous—and these flowers…did you arrange them?"

"Every. Last. One."

"Breathtaking! So perfect for tonight. I love them."

"You deserve nothing but the best, my darling. Let me go find a place to set them down, and I'll be right back."

"Wait, where's Mirabelle?" asked Maeve.

"She's coming in behind me. Last I heard, she was on the phone with Grandma, giving her an ultimatum."

"What kind of ultimatum?"

"Something about not spoiling the twins by letting them stay up late to watch television...or eat dairy...or breathe. I don't know, I don't understand Chinese." Christopher rolled his eyes and sashayed off to find the perfect place to display his handiwork.

"That's our Mirabelle!" laughed Maeve.

"*Māmā, méiyôu!*" Mirabelle marched in, on her cell phone, continuing to reprimand her mother in a language neither Maeve nor Rochelle understood. She ended her call with a huff, placed her phone into her beaded evening bag, and inhaled a long, deep breath. Exhaling slowly, she opened her arms and said, "Fuck it! Ladies, let's get this party started. Where's the booze?"

Maeve laughed. Rochelle shook her head, "Good God, I love you Mirabelle."

Mirabelle handed her silk-wrapped gift to Rochelle. "Love you too, Ro, happy birthday."

HARRY'S ARRIVAL

C hristopher parted Waterford luminaries, settling his extravagant arrangement onto the circular Chippendale mahogany table nestled in the alcove beneath the curved staircase in Rochelle's grand foyer. He meticulously maneuvered stems and leaves so each exquisite bloom would be showcased to all who entered. He stood back, running fingers through his thick, chocolate waves as he assessed his creation. It was that exact moment a flustered Harry burst through the front door.

"Oh my God, how can I compete with that?"

"Jesus, Marty, and Joseph! You scared the daylights out of me." Christopher turned, clutching his imaginary pearls

"Sorry...there was a catering truck blocking the driveway. Rochelle is going to kill me for being so late." Harry looked handsome in his Tom Ford suit and tie. His sandy hair was a bit disheveled, but it only added to his effortless good looks.

With a crinkled brow, Christopher judged the floral arrangement Harry held in his right hand. "Sweetheart, I'd leave that Walmart mess on the front porch." He spied a small velvet box in Harry's other hand, "However, I'm sure whatever bauble is in *that* box will do."

"Fuck, Chris! I completely forgot it was Rochelle's birthday! My secretary reminded me at the last minute. I had to run to the jeweler, and traffic was a nightmare." Harry opened the front door and tossed the mundane floral arrangement into the front bushes. Closing the door, he brushed his hair back and straightened his jacket.

Christopher shook his head, "I don't know how she puts up with your antics."

"Me neither. I can't keep up with my own."

"Well, you'd better start groveling...oh, and the gang's all here, so it's showtime."

Harry grumbled as he and Christopher made their way to the bar where they were met by a room rife with chatter as the aroma of good food lingered in the air.

ROCHELLE CAUGHT her breath as Harry entered the room. The pink dagger previously plunged through her heart now twisted in place at the sight of her husband. His atrocity suddenly seemed all too real. Unable to decipher if it was anxiety or indignation, the sour in the pit of her stomach bubbled, tickling the back of her throat. She swallowed hard and reminded herself to stay the course.

"Well, look what the cat dragged in," Barrington bellowed. His voice always a bit too loud at all the wrong moments.

"Hey everyone," Harry addressed the crowd and made a sheepish beeline toward his wife. "Happy birthday, Ro," he leaned down to give Rochelle a kiss, his back to the crowd, and whispered, "I'm sorry."

Rochelle averted her face ever so slightly so no one would notice —he didn't deserve her lips. Instead, she envisioned herself removing her platinum hair comb and plunging it deep into his chest. Harry handed the black velvet box to Rochelle who—without a second glance—placed it on the credenza next to her other gifts. Her eyes dared Harry to comment.

Rochelle noticed Maeve and Mirabelle glance at each other and then back at her—the unspoken code in the world of close female friendships. They can read each other's minds, women. They instinctively know when something is wrong. They also know when to address it and when to let it go. This was a time to let it go.

"I'll open presents later." Rochelle feigned happiness. "I'd rather spend time with all of you first." She left Harry standing there and moved closer to her friends. Christopher peered over his glasses, sipping his martini, taking note of Harry's flushed cheeks.

"Let's make a toast to the birthday girl!" Barrington cut through the tension, and for once Rochelle was glad he was taking control of the conversation. He held the now-opened bottle of hundred-year-old scotch in his hand and gave it to the bartender. "My good man, pour a glass for everyone!"

The bartender did as he was told. Barrington lifted two glasses from the bar, handing one to both Harry and Rochelle, while everyone else helped themselves.

"Thanks, just a sip," Rochelle accepted the glass from Barrington, "I'm not drinking this evening." She glanced over at the bartender, who did not look up, nor acknowledge the comment she knew he'd heard. *Good boy.*

The friends hoisted their glasses higher, toasting Rochelle. Rochelle raised the drink to her lips and sipped...the aged alcohol stung her nostrils. "Time for dinner. Shall we all gather in the dining room?"

DINNER WITH THE HAWTHORNES

I t came in like a lion—the argument. Actually, it came in with the lamb and—most likely—several glasses of hundred-year-old scotch. One moment guests were oohing and aahing over the three-foot crystal candelabras, arranged to illuminate the exquisite table-scape, and the next they were boozily embattled in politics and social issues over rack of lamb served with brown butter radishes and carrot soufflé.

"Oh my God, Barrington! I'm just saying that the president's proposed sanctions on China are ridiculous." Mirabelle pointed across the table with her fork to make her four-pronged point.

"Ridiculous?" Never one to turn down an argument, or a good meal, Barrington mopped up some carrot puree with a lamb chop and stuck it in his mouth, managing to gnaw it off the bone and speak all at the same time. "It's about time other countries started paying." He chewed through his words. "They've been taking advantage of us for far too long. Look at how our economy is booming."

Maeve tried to change the conversation. "This lamb is amazin', Rochelle." She knew her husband all too well, and he wasn't about to lose an argument—especially about politics—especially with a woman, "and this soufflé, it's to die for."

Rochelle was starting to feel the effects of the alcohol she'd drunk earlier; she managed a squint and a smile.

"This is not going to end well, you know why?" Mirabelle kept on.

"Tell me, why?" Barrington dared, spreading herbed butter onto a knotted dinner roll.

"Because both leaders are stubborn. Each thinks their own country's economic prowess will force the other over a barrel."

"Bah! I'm sure the president wants to force *someone* over a barrel," Christopher joked "but she'd probably have to be in her early twenties."

Mirabelle snickered. Rochelle tried to salt her lamb chop.

"What's that supposed to mean?" Barrington asked, stuffing the dinner roll into his mouth.

"You know what it means. He's a horn-dog, a pervert, all he's thinking about is the next intern he can bang." All wide eyes were on Christopher, who added, "Heil, Commander Asshat."

Rochelle shook the saltshaker, but nothing came out.

"Chris—" Harry started in, but Barrington quickly cut him off.

"How dare you disrespect your president like that?"

Maeve patted her husband's arm, a silent signal for him to shut it down.

Rochelle placed her hand under the saltshaker and shook again. No salt.

"Not MY president, Barry! He doesn't respect me or who I love. Why should I respect him?"

Rochelle loosened the cap to the saltshaker.

"It's Barrington! And who *do* you love *Chrissy?*"

"Oh, OK, settle down, *Barrington!*" Mirabelle's inner dragon came to her friend's defense. "Your hidden homophobe is showing!"

"I'm not a homophobe, and maybe you should move back to China if you don't like how it's going here. Isn't that where all your properties are, anyway?"

"Barrington Avery Spencer!" Maeve squeezed her husband's arm —hard.

"Ow!" He yanked his arm away from his wife's talons.

Rochelle tried to be careful, but the top of the shaker popped off and a mound of salt poured onto her plate.

"God!" Christopher continued, "Who do I love?"

"Chris..." Harry tried once again to settle his friends.

Rochelle drank her water. *I need something stronger than this.*

"How thickskulled can you closed-minded conservatives be? All you care about is money. Always deflecting by talking about *us*, like we choose our sexuality. I'll tell you who I love."

"Chris..."

"It's not a choice, you inconsiderate bigot. I love who I love."

"Christopher!" Harry yelled, banging on the table with flat palms, causing the china and sterling silver to rattle in his wake. "Stop arguing!" The room fell silent. Harry appeared to regain his composure. "Everyone..." he forced out the breath he'd inhaled, "tonight we are celebrating Rochelle, and we are *not* going to have a political debate at this table!"

No one said a word. Rochelle started to laugh, as she stared at the mound of salt covering her lamb. She laughed—long and disturbed, as she raised her gaze to Harry. She laughed until tears replaced the glaze in her eyes. She laughed until she cried.

This is not how she envisioned her plan playing out, but it was too late now. The effects of the two martinis and the valium made her arms feel numb. Her body buzzed. Her inner voice screamed to be set free. She pushed her salt-laden plate aside and grabbed her champagne glass filled with water, as she stood at the foot of her dining room table, holding the edge with one hand to steady herself, mascara puddled underneath her verdigris-colored eyes. She clinked the Waterford flute with her fork. Her four friends and her lying husband slowly raised their glasses to join in. Elegant and innocent, beautiful in her Old Hollywood attire, unpracticed at vengeance, she looked deep into Harry's eyes.

"I'm pregnant."

～

THROUGH GASPS from her delighted friends, Rochelle watched a stunned Harry shrink at his end of the table. She thought she could hear the candles sizzling, wax surrendering to the heat, as flames scorched the wicks, turning them from white to black, just like Harry's aura.

Rochelle walked to Harry's end of the table as he slowly rose from his seat, dabbing his forehead with his monogrammed linen napkin before tossing it aside. Rochelle wrapped her arms around his waist and raised her crimson lips close to his ear, heavily whispering, "Surpriiise." Harry sat back down, awestruck.

"Oh my goodness, honeybee," Maeve squealed, "congratulations!" She stood to give Rochelle hug. Rochelle clung to Maeve, still staring at Harry, who was now downing his scotch. Rochelle hoped Maeve wouldn't notice the slight waver in her stance—she was surprised how strong two secret martinis and one tiny valium on an empty stomach could actually be. "That's why you weren't drinking?" Maeve then frowned at her husband, "Barrington, apologize to Rochelle."

"I'm sorry, Rochelle." Barrington turned to Harry, "Congrats, my good man." He shook Harry's hand. "Holy Toledo! Your hand feels like a dead fish on a hot and humid August afternoon. Relax! You've got nine months to prepare!"

Rochelle watched a pallid Harry squirm in his skin. It was the exact reaction she'd hoped for. Although, she wished her focus wasn't as fuzzy. It would have been delightful to have a crystal clear view of his uneasiness.

"This calls for a celebratory round!" Barrington boomed, looking around for the bartender who was nowhere in sight, "Christopher, can you grab that bottle near you and pour us all another scotch?"

Christopher lifted the bottle and made his way around the table, filling everyone's glasses. "Congratulations," he said, as he leaned down, filling Harry's glass. Harry shot the scotch immediately.

Mirabelle held out her glass and shook it, summoning Christopher. As Christopher poured, Mirabelle's cell rang, "Hello? Mama. What? I said NO television!" Mirabelle turned to Christopher, "We've got to go, this woman is incompetent!" Mirabelle rose from her seat, "My sincere apologies, Rochelle, the girls have math camp in the morning. I promise I'll make it up to you." She blew Rochelle a kiss and exited the room, yelling at her mother in Chinese.

"We're going to finish our conversationnn..." Barrington called out after her.

Mirabelle flipped him the bird as she, and the clack of her high heels, disappeared down the long hallway.

Christopher stood, embarrassed, holding the bottle of scotch. "Well, thanks for an...um...eventful evening, and...uh...happy birthday, Rochelle, and...congratulations," he said, taking the scotch with him as he scurried out after Mirabelle.

9

DIGGING IN THE DIRT

Rochelle opened one eye as Moosh licked her awake, the delicate breath from his little nostrils tickling her face. Afraid to make any quick movements, she tried to assess the probable severity of her hangover, fearful a wave of nausea or an ice pick to the brain would be her morning greeting. As she opened her other eye, and rustled just enough to give her sweet pup a scratch, she realized none of that was going to happen. Other than a severe case of cottonmouth and an overwhelming desire to sleep, she was free and clear of any morning's sickness.

Morning Sickness! Rochelle rolled over to address Harry, to have the conversation they didn't have last night. Harry's drinking into the wee hours with Barrington put an end to that. Now, his rumpled side of the bed was cold and empty, his abandoned sheet in disarray. She looked at the clock, shocked it was almost noon. She pushed herself out of bed and slid into her slippers, quickly pulling her fiery mane into a messy bun on top of her head, feeling the coolness of the air-condition-ing on her now-exposed neck.

Rochelle carried Moosh, along with her depression, into the kitchen where the remnants of toast and old early morning coffee hung in the air. She unlocked the doggie door and let her little buddy scamper out into the yard to do his business. Still, no Harry. In his place, next to the plate of unfinished scrambled eggs, was a note in his handwriting. *Had to run...talk later. H-*

Is he kidding? Rochelle crumpled the paper, irked at how after last night's shocking, albeit false, announcement, Harry could possibly have the indecency to leave the house before having a conversation. Tension knotted her chest as she poured what was left of the over-warmed coffee into a mug and took a sip, its bitterness dehydrating her palate even more. She imagined the overwhelming bitterness she held inside for Harry would do the same to her soul. Abandoning the mug, she opted instead to fill a large glass with ice, and reached into the Sub-Zero for a bottle of sparkling water.

With the slightest tremor in her hand, she poured the water over crystal clear ice cubes, watching it flow, as the carbonation popped and fizzed, shushing her chaotic thoughts. Tiny chilled bubbles erupted, kissing her face as she drank. She welcomed in the cold cleansing liquid, gulping it down before filling her glass again, hoping to clear the overindulgence from her system, wishing it would also clear her mind.

Moosh scampered back into the kitchen, and Rochelle placed the plate of scrambled eggs on the floor for him. The hungry pup devoured the food in no time, reminding Rochelle of her own hunger. Her hunger for a child—one she kept hidden deep in her soul. One that Harry refused to satiate.

Thoughts screaming, she longed for stillness, and knew of only one place to find it.

THE SEARING TEXAS sun pulsed high in the sky as Rochelle's gloveless hands found solace in the cool dirt. The incessant heat on her back did not bother her, it felt like the warm hand of God pressing on her, keeping her safe from her own thoughts. This was her happy place, her garden.

It was cathartic, squeezing the earth between bare hands—a meditation of sorts, as she attempted to push Harry and his lies out of her mind. A symphony of cicadas provided her soundtrack. The hotter it got, the louder their vibrations became. The stuttering sound of the insects' mating calls reminded Rochelle of the sound of rattlesnakes. Her mind's eye visualized multiple serpents twisted and tangled around branches, high in the trees, looking down, shaking their threatening tails at the world below.

Harry was a snake. A lying, deceitful, fork-tongued reptile who slithered away like the coward he was, avoiding the inevitable conversation. Rochelle's confused mind ached with questions. Why did he betray her like this? What went through his mind? She needed to know. The effects of her overindulgence made it too hard for her to focus last night. She'd overdone it. She hated herself for that—not being all there. Plus, Harry would have been of no use to her, drinking congratulatory shots of Don Julio Real with Barrington well into the night, before stumbling into bed. Now he was off, hiding from her. He didn't answer her calls. Was he trying to figure out what to say? What lie to make up? Would he pretend to be happy? Or would he confess his secret pink sin? It didn't matter anyway. She needed time to think.

Rochelle scooped a mound of dirt from the garden bed, making a hole, just the way the revelation of Harry's vasectomy scooped out her heart. She filled the hole with a red-leafed begonia and smoothed the surrounding dirt over its roots, tucking it in with care. She thought she could smell the alcohol sweating from her skin as it dripped into the soil, becoming one with the earth. Why didn't Harry want children the way she so desperately did? She looked up to see Moosh, under the shade of an old Live Oak, gnawing on a small branch he'd found. She was thankful for him, for filling the void in her heart, in as good a way as a dog could replace a child.

Rochelle wanted so desperately to have a baby. All these years, she thought her body was broken and goddamned Harry didn't disagree with that. She remembered the time she sobbed to him, curled up on the couch, five years into their marriage, as Harry sat and listened.

～

"IT'S OK, ROCHELLE," Harry stroked her hair away from her teary eyes, as her head lay on his lap.

"I'm such a failure, Harry," she sobbed, "I thought by now we'd be pregnant again. I wanted so much to have your children...to have our children."

"It's not your fault your body couldn't hold a baby, Ro. It doesn't make you any less of a woman."

"But, why?" she wailed. "Why me? I would be such a good mother. I've got everything to give."

"You would, Rochelle...and you do. It's just not in the cards for us."

A long silence held their attention, the ticking of Harry's wristwatch filled the chasm. Second after second clicked by, echoing, reminding Rochelle of her biological clock. Rochelle sat up suddenly and wiped the tears from her eyes onto the sleeve of her sweatshirt. "Maybe it is."

"Maybe *what* is?"

"Having a baby...in the cards for us...we can always adopt."

"Oh...I don't know about that, babe."

"What do you mean you don't know about it?"

"I don't know," Harry crossed his arms in subconscious defense, "I'm not keen on raising someone else's kid."

"Oh my God, Harry, it wouldn't be someone else's child. It would be ours! An infant, to raise right from the beginning of its life."

"How do we know where they came from? What if the mother was a drug addict? Or the father was an alcoholic? I don't know."

"Harry..."

"I'd rather it be my own genes, or none at all."

"But we'd have so much to offer a child who doesn't have their own par—"

"Rochelle!" Harry stood from the sofa, "I'm done talking about this. I have so much going on at work...too much to focus on right now. I just can't think about this!"

"I'm sorry." Rochelle crumpled, feeling bad for being selfish, for pushing her desires onto her husband, when all he was trying to do was work hard to provide for both of them.

"It's OK, just don't bring it up again…"

"Sorry…" she whispered.

She never did.

Dirt from her hands smudged her face as Rochelle wiped away her falling tears. She scooped out another mound of earth and set her hand shovel aside. Reaching deep into the pocket of her gardening apron, she pulled out the folded pink paper. She unfolded the paper and began to tear it up into tiny pieces, slowly at first, and then faster and faster. In a fit of uncontrollable rage, she tore the paper to shreds while she wailed from the depths of her pain.

Into the hole, she mashed Harry's horrible secret. Her palms, grinding it into the earth with all her might, along with the idea of him, of him calling to make the appointment. The appointment that would change the course of their life together.

Rochelle smushed, into the earth, the fact that Harry'd had a vasectomy, without her knowledge, without her blessing and three years *before* having the conversation about Rochelle's broken body, her selfishness, and the adoption she was to never bring up again.

She knelt on the ground and squeezed with all her shaking might the now soiled shreds of Harry's sins against her as she sobbed, rocking back and forth, collapsing to the ground, exhausted and defeated. Moosh ran over and delicately licked Rochelle's salty, dirty, tear-streaked face. The patient pup laid by Rochelle's face, intently watching her closed eyes, until Rochelle regained her composure.

With dirty hands, soil packed deep under her nails, Rochelle pushed herself up to her knees, and brushed frazzled strands of hair away from her face as she cleared her throat and sniffled. Into the battered hole, sprinkled with torn remnants of Harry's unforgivable secret, Rochelle placed another red-leaf begonia. She pushed the surrounding dirt to cover the roots, nestling them in ever so carefully.

As she patted the top of the soil, in the heat of the Texas sun, God's warm hand on her back, to the symphony of cicadas, she made a decision. She no longer wanted a conversation with her lying husband, she no longer needed to know, nor cared, what he was thinking. There was a better solution. *Harry needed to die.*

10

MOOSH

P*resent day...*

With the garden center far behind her, the tires of Rochelle's car crunched and crackled through the bucolic countryside as she wondered just how she was going to kill Harry. She was obviously good at planning things, down to the very last detail. But not this, this was different, uncharacteristically spontaneous. After what Harry had done. She fought to pull herself together as she slowed to a stop at the quiet intersection where country meets city and made her way onto the highway.

Hours passed like minutes and she found herself turning into the front driveway of her Highland Park estate, unable to remember the drive back. Magically transported—possibly by UFO, one that adorns the T-shirt of a teenage conspiracy theorist begrudgingly working at a remote garden center.

She sat in her car for a moment, taking in a long, deep breath as her cramped hands gripped the wheel. Rochelle scanned her home through the windshield of her SUV. Her impressive stone estate looked so peaceful—romantic, sheltered behind three giant Live Oak trees on the lazy street in her ritzy Dallas suburb. This was her neighborhood, where one mansion was bigger than the next.

Sometimes, on the weekends, she would watch as outsiders drove by. She could tell they didn't belong by the cars they drove, cars of lesser value, dented and bruised. They'd slowly roll through, street after street, passengers and drivers alike, gawking in awe out of their car windows, impressed by the beautiful homes they could only dream of owning. From the outside, the fastidiously manicured mansions spoke of perfect lives, lives of greater value. Little did the visitors know that inside the opulent facades lived a very different story. For inside the decadent mansions, people were dented and bruised just like the curious cars.

Rochelle didn't bother pulling through the porte cochere into the courtyard this time. She'd leave her car right there, exactly where she wanted. Harry always complained when she left her car in the driveway, hated to have to wait for her to move it when he had somewhere important to be. Everything Harry did was important, he'd always talk about his important business meetings with important businesspeople discussing important business things. He'd be irate if five minutes of his important time was spent waiting for Rochelle to back out of the driveway. His importance always made her feel less than...unimportant. She left her car in the driveway and excavated her bag of supplies.

Rochelle knew Harry had an early, most likely important, meeting and would already be gone. They still hadn't discussed her pregnancy announcement. Once she'd made up her mind to...to end things...she avoided Harry altogether. Making herself busy late into the evening until she knew he would be in bed. She even slept on the sofa last night. Harry didn't seem to notice. As he entered the kitchen earlier this morning, Rochelle was gathering her purse, keys, and sunglasses, preparing to make her run to the garden center.

"Morning," Harry said as he grabbed the coffeepot and poured himself a cup.

"Morning." Rochelle wouldn't look at him.

"You're up early."

"Yep...things to do. Keep an eye on Moosh, I'll be back in a bit." She was out the door in a flash.

Now she was back, Harry was gone, and once inside, she would make a cup of tea, cuddle with Moosh, and fantasize Harry's demise.

She could hear her dog yip just beyond the door as she rustled her key into the lock with one hand while holding her bag of supplies in the other.

"Coming, Moosh! Mommy's home!" As the door swung open, her little dog ran to greet her. It took a minute for it to register—the blood on the pup's paws and underbelly.

"Oh my God! Moosh!" Rochelle dropped her bag, splaying its contents on the floor. "What happened to you?" She pulled a towel from the scattered supplies as she reached for her little dog. He yipped again as she quickly scooped him up, wrapping him tightly in the towel, immobilizing him. Afraid to look for the injury, she placed the swaddled pup into her oversized handbag and ran to her car. Carefully, she settled him on the passenger seat and buckled the seat belt around the bag before quickly backing out of her driveway, narrowly missing the man walking his German shepherd.

ROCHELLE BURST through the doors of the emergency veterinarian's office with Moosh in her arms as the blue-haired receptionist rose from behind the desk.

"Please, help me! Something's happened to my dog!"

A veterinary assistant quickly emerged from the back, summoned by the commotion. "There, there, let's take a look at this wee one."

Rochelle carefully handed her bag, with a wrapped and immobilized Moosh to the technician; only the dog's snout was exposed. The rest of his body was tightly bound in the white terry towel. The pup whimpered.

"Please! I don't know what's happened!"

"I'll take him back to Dr. H, please have a seat."

"But, I want to be with him." Rochelle tried to follow the technician, who carried Moosh into the back room. The receptionist came around to intercept and compassionately took Rochelle by the arm.

"Dr. Herzog will call you into the back, dear. Let them examine your dog. Come. Sit." Rochelle obeyed her commands. Apparently, they worked on humans just as well.

Minutes passed like hours, Rochelle rose from the hard plastic chair, trying not to burn her lip on the hot tea as her trembling hand created a turbulent herbal storm, threatening scalding waves to crash against her upper lip. She blew hot steam over Styrofoam—she hated Styrofoam, it gave her teeth the chills. She loved that little dog. He was her baby, and the closest thing to a child she would ever have. There was no calming her. She paced like a caged animal and tried to sip anyway. She burned her lip. "Shit!"

Blue-hair, now on the phone, gave her a stern look from behind the desk and glanced at the chair next to Rochelle in the empty waiting area. Rochelle sat again.

It wasn't long before Dr. Herzog emerged from the back room. The plump man with brown skin and kind eyes summoned Rochelle. Rochelle hyper-focused on the tiny blood stains littering his white lab coat.

"How is he, Doctor?" A jolt of adrenaline flushed her face.

"Follow me, Mrs. Hawthorne."

Dread blanketed Rochelle as she placed the Styrofoam cup onto the reception desk and followed the doctor into one of the examination rooms. It smelled of wet animal and flea powder. Moosh wasn't there.

"What's wrong with Moosh, Doctor? Where is he?"

"He's in the other room, Mrs. Hawthorne. They're cleaning him up."

"What's wrong with him? What happened to him?"

"Where did you say you found him, Mrs. Hawthorne?"

"He was in the house when I got home."

"Does he have a way to get out of the house when you're not home?"

"Yes, a doggy door leading to the back yard."

"Ahhh…I see," replied the doctor, scribbling something onto a chart.

"What's wrong with him?"

"Nothing."

A pause.

"What?" She was confused.

"There's nothing wrong with your dog, Mrs. Hawthorne."

"But...the blood..."

"It isn't your dog's blood."

11

SO MUCH FOR PLANNING

Rochelle turned into her driveway with a content, and unharmed, Moosh on her lap. She was relieved her fur-baby was OK, didn't know what she would do if anything happened to him. She pushed the dreaded thought out of her mind.

She picked up her pup, settling multiple kisses on his damp head as she walked toward the door. She must have left it ajar in her rush to get Moosh to the vet. It was already 3:30 in the afternoon. Dr. Herzog explained Moosh must have run out through the doggie door and caught a squirrel or another small animal in the back yard. She nodded in agreement with the doctor but was confused. Moosh always chased the squirrels and bunnies in the yard, but never actually caught one. And if he did, Rochelle couldn't imagine him ravaging the animal.

This was Harry's fault. Why wouldn't he crate Moosh before he left for the day? She should have taken the dog with her, but she didn't want to be distracted from her list. Now she was left to clean up the mess. She was done cleaning up Harry's messes.

The happy pup licked Rochelle's face as she pushed open the door. "Mommy loves you too, baby." She kissed the dog again and set him down. "Ugh." The items from her shopping trip were scattered about, along with faint bloody paw prints spread across the white marble floor. She grabbed the container of bleach from the floor and another of the towels she bought that morning, and headed toward her kitchen. Moosh trailed behind her, his tail wagging. She turned to the dog. "Good boy, Moosh! Mommy'll give you a treat before she cleans up this mess."

The little dog stopped before the doorway to the kitchen, panting at her. Rochelle stood beneath the arched entrance. "C'mon, baby!" The dog wouldn't enter. "C'mon, Moosh! Treat!" Moosh sat. "OK, have it your way."

Rochelle approached the large apron sink, plugged the drain and turned on the water. Acrid fumes stung her nose as she poured a bit of bleach and tossed in the towel. She headed toward the mud room at the back of the kitchen for the mop, when her right foot met with something wet, causing it to slide. She looked down at the crimson puddle. It didn't register at first. Frozen, her heartbeat pounded in her chest as her eyes followed the flow, followed it slowly across the white, Italian marble, followed it to the base of the large, kitchen island. The island that previously hid Harry's body, lying on the floor, in a pool of his own blood. She didn't recognize her own scream.

As for her plan? Someone else beat her to it

12

911

The living room walls shrunk in around Rochelle as the officer asked her questions. She watched his mouth, tried to focus through a blur of tears, as it moved in slow motion. She zeroed in on the tiny chip in his front tooth as he spoke. She tried to concentrate. What was he saying?

"I know this is difficult, Mrs. Hawthorne, but I have a few questions, if it's OK with you?" Rochelle didn't answer as she rocked back and forth, grasping Moosh tight to her chest. The officer continued.

"When was the last time you spoke to your husband?"

"Uh...uhm...this morning before I left." She wondered how he'd chipped his tooth.

"You left to go where?"

"Shopping." Rochelle remembered the bird, trapped in the garden center, tapping away at the glass. *Flutter-flutter, tip-tap.* She envisioned the bird chipping away at the officer's front tooth.

"What were you shopping for?" Other than that small divot, his teeth were perfect.

Murder cleanup supplies. "Uh...gardening supplies." She watched the officer scribble on his notepad.

"What was his mood when you left the house?"

"Uh...I...I don't know. It was...normal, I guess." The flapping of the bird's wings in Rochelle's head made it hard for her to hear the officer. She rocked harder trying to soothe herself.

"Did you and your husband have an argument this morning?"

"No."

"Do you know of anyone who would want to harm your husband, Mrs. Hawthorne?"

I would. "No."

～

"Sorry to interrupt, Detective Blankenship, but we're finished here."

"Thank you."

The officer questioning Rochelle thanked the man in the white jumpsuit. There were a few of them, both men and women, in white jumpsuits now stained with Harry's blood. This jumpsuit must have been the leader, for as he spoke to the officer, the rest of the jumpsuits carried things out of Rochelle's house. Things tucked inside large brown paper bags and sealed with red tape printed over and over with the word *evidence.*

Rochelle wondered what was in the bags. Was it the breakfast plate she saw, split in two, lying next to her husband, with not a remnant of scrambled eggs left? Rochelle knew there were once scrambled eggs on that plate, something Harry made for himself every morning. Was the fork Harry used to eat the eggs in a bag? Why would the jumpsuits take a fork? Would an intruder have touched it before stabbing her husband? *I wonder if they'll give that back?* Rochelle stressed over the thought of an incomplete set. She knew her set of Wüsthof kitchen knives were in a bag, because apparently one of them was missing from the block. Probably the one that was slid in and out of her husband's flesh, rendering him immobile. She wondered what else the white jumpsuits were carrying out of her house. She hadn't been in her kitchen since...she could only imagine.

She wondered what the white jumpsuits thought, looking at her dead husband lying on her kitchen floor, his blood seeping into the thin grout lines between the once pristine Italian marble. She wondered what they thought as they casually glanced at her, the grieving widow, sitting on her sage nubuck sofa, being questioned by the officer with the chip in his tooth, as they tucked the supplies from her shopping trip —the murder cleanup supplies, into large brown paper bags.

She wondered what the officer thought as he questioned her, pretending to be casual, but most likely thinking she was the stabber. She had an idea of his thoughts. For as his mouth moved in slow motion, his eyes did as well, carefully taking in every ounce of her being, all while writing in his notebook. *Flutter-flutter tip-tap.* She saw him analyze her posture and her body language. Was she open or closed? She saw him scan her hands as she held onto Moosh's warm body for comfort. Were they possibly wielding a knife just moments before? Were her palms bruised and pink with the force it took to stab Harry...*if* she had actually been the stabber?

"Mrs. Hawthorne, it's getting late, but I was wondering if you'd accompany me to the station where I can get an official statement from you?"

Rochelle wondered if the white jumpsuits and the officer took a good look at Harry as he lay on the floor, dead in his kitchen, next to his empty broken plate of invisible scrambled eggs. Could they see what a liar he was? Could they tell he betrayed her in the most selfish, heartless way...murdering every ounce of Rochelle's happiness?

"OK, sure."

Flutter-flutter, tip tap

13

DEPRESSION

Two days and one death later, Rochelle lay on her bed with Moosh snuggled up next to her as she twirled the little white curls on top of his head. It was soothing—the tactile caressing of something soft. The pup emanated more heat than his small body should have been capable of. She didn't mind. She longed for warmth, for lately, a constant chill inhabited her. It was Tuesday afternoon, and the sun was forcing slivers of itself through the closed wooden shutters in her bedroom, pleading her awake. Yes, she longed for warmth, but wouldn't dare let it in—afraid the sun would illuminate the monster hiding in the dark. She even let her phone battery die so the screen would not light. She lay in the bed, in the same pajamas she'd worn for days, teeth not brushed, body not bathed, clinging to the only thing she had left to love in the world, trying to sleep off the nightmare she hoped she was stuck in.

It was two days. Two days after she fantasized about getting rid of Harry. Two days after actually finding him, stabbed multiple times and lying in a pool of his own blood, on their kitchen floor. Did she will this into being? Was the power of her anger strong enough to force the universe into a series of unfortunate events, eventually leading to her husband's demise? Did her inner thoughts slice through his skin in real time, as forceful as the rage that thrashed inside her? Was it her fault he was dead? The police thought so.

After her trip to the emergency vet with Moosh, the rest of that bloody Sunday was a blur. She remembered wanting to clean up Moosh's bloody paw prints, remembered opening the bleach. She recalled slipping on something, seeing the trail of blood, and, eventually, Harry on the floor. She did not remember calling 911. Yet, there were officers with her, asking questions in her shrinking living room. Then, at the police station, there were more questions from Detective Blankenship—a lot of questions. She recalled bits and pieces.

"Mrs. Hawthorne, can I get you some water?"

"Yes, please."

The detective handed Rochelle a bottle of water as she sat in the interrogation room. "Mrs. Hawthorne, once again, I'm very sorry for your loss."

My loss? If only you knew what I have lost—all those years. The last eight years when Harry and I—when I, could have had a child. Those were taken away from me. Harry took those away from me! That's what I have lost! "Thank you for the water."

Rochelle's head hurt recalling what felt like scene after scene of continual questions in the interrogation room at the police station.

"Mrs. Hawthorne, why did you pour bleach into your sink? Were you trying to clean the area?"

"I wanted to clean Moosh's footpri—wait, where's Moosh?"

"Moosh?"

"My dog."

"Oh, he's with, uhm," the detective glanced at his notes, "with a Maeve Spencer. We asked you if you had someone you could call, and you called Mrs. Spencer."

"Oh," Rochelle didn't remember calling Maeve.

"Was that before or after you found your husband?"

"I'm sorry?"

"You wanting to clean up. Before or after you discovered your husband?"

"It was before. I wanted to clean up the paw prints. I found Harry when I went to get the mop."

"Didn't you think it was odd your dog was bloody when you came home? That there were bloody paw prints on the floor?"

"No...uhm...yes, but I wasn't thinking, I just panicked."

"About the blood?"

"About the dog—about getting him to the vet, I don't know what I'd do if I lost him."

"Your husband?"

She didn't want to relive the memories—didn't want to think at all, but her mind wouldn't stop racing. It wouldn't stop going back to two days ago. Rochelle hugged Moosh closer to her chest as she lay in her bed, maybe she'd never leave this spot, maybe she'd die here. She closed her eyes tighter but a sliver of light pushed itself through the blinds, at just the right angle. From inside herself, she saw inside of her illuminated eyelid, the part that stays hidden from the outside world —it looked bright red. It reminded her of the blood. The blood on Moosh, the blood on Harry, the blood on her kitchen floor—a kitchen she hadn't stepped into in two days. Nothing was going to make her enter that kitchen again.

Well, nothing short of blood.

14

LOSS

On her knees, Rochelle scrubbed furiously at the thin grout lines running between the Italian marble slabs on her kitchen floor. Still in her pajamas, teeth unbrushed, body unbathed, and from the looks of her reflection in the mirror she passed, blazing hair matted and mangled.

The cleanup crew was called in after the event—she had the bill to prove it. But their job was unsatisfactory. Did they not even attempt to clean to the grout? Did they not see the brown shadows that remained?

Rochelle remembered seeing the thin brown lines when she was allowed to return home, when detective What's-His-Name escorted her back. He told her the cleanup crew had done their job, that her beautiful home was no longer an ugly crime scene. So back she went. She no longer saw Moosh's little prints trailing all over the foyer. But, in the kitchen, in the fine grout lines, where one marble slab was carefully nestled to the next, there was blood.

"There's no blood, Mrs. Hawthorne," said the detective.

"I see blood right there," she insisted.

"Right where?"

"There," Rochelle pointed, "in plain sight, in the cracks."

The detective tried to assure her the chemicals used were potent and sufficient. Rochelle thought otherwise. It dawned on her, as she lay with Moosh in her bed, trying to consign to oblivion the events of recent days. She was never going to be able to forget the event. Especially not if the thin brown lines were still in existence.

With Moosh in his crate, she got to work. Donning yellow dish gloves, she dipped an old toothbrush into bleach and started to scrub the grout, carefully making sure to cover all the places she thought were tainted. After a while, she stood back to examine her work—still, there were thin, brown lines. The toothbrush was not working, it was probably too soft.

Rochelle rummaged through a kitchen drawer to find something thinner, sharper—a box cutter. It was printed with a logo for Magic Movers, the company that moved Rochelle and Harry into their Highland Park estate, eight-and-a-half years ago. As she fastidiously scraped the blade down the length of each grout line, she remembered the day.

It was a year and a half into their marriage and they were moving from New York to Dallas. Dallas was booming and the perfect place to add another branch to Harry's growing tech company. Harry was back in New York for a meeting and wouldn't be arriving in Texas until the following day. Rochelle asked him to reschedule, she knew how picky Harry was and thought it better he be with her to help manage the movers. But Harry refused, saying his meeting was more important, leaving Rochelle to manage the movers on her own.

She flew in the night before the movers were to arrive, took a taxi to the house, and slept on the carpeted floor of the master bedroom, in order to be available first thing in the morning, just in case the truck arrived earlier than expected. She was tired, unable to sleep the night before, she'd waited for the sun to rise, eager to get to work unpacking and organizing. It was something she loved to do. She was also three months pregnant. It was the one and only time she would ever get to be genuinely happy.

The movers arrived and started to wheel boxes into the expansive home, unloading their dollies, placing marked cardboard containers everywhere, as Rochelle directed them into the appropriate rooms.

Soon, furniture, boxes and crates filled the entire space. It was almost overwhelming, the sea of clutter before her, but Rochelle knew she was capable of handling the task of unpacking their belongings. Organizing things calmed her.

Four hours later, just as the movers were dropping the last of the boxes, Harry called.

"Hey babe, how's it going?"

"Hi…it's going," Rochelle sat on the plastic-wrapped couch to take a load off her swollen feet. It was the first time she sat all day. Her lower back was starting to ache and she was hungry. "I wish you were here, there's a lot of work to be done. They're almost finished unloading." She brushed loose hair strands away from her face.

"I'll be there soon enough…early morning."

"Good, because there are boxes everywhere, it'll go fast with the two of us working together."

"Boxes? They are supposed to do a full unpack," Harry sounded annoyed, "supposed to remove all the contents and take the boxes and paper with them."

"No, I spoke to the foreman," Rochelle didn't like confrontation and wasn't about to argue with a gruff mover, "they are just dropping boxes. He said that's what's on the work order."

"Rochelle…the contract was for them to unpack *all* of the boxes and take the garbage with them."

"Harry, it's not a problem. I can manage."

Harry was indignant. "Put the guy on the phone, Rochelle!"

Rochelle handed the phone to the stone-faced foreman and could hear Harry yelling at him on the other end. Rochelle was embarrassed, for herself, for Harry, and for the mover who hung up the phone with a frown and handed it back to her. "OK, lady, we have two hours left to try to unpack all of these boxes…after that we're off the clock."

With that, the movers started storming through Rochelle's and Harry's precious belongings. Box cutters marked Miracle Movers were slashing through cardboard as unhappy, unorganized men were just placing things everywhere and anywhere. It was overwhelming for Rochelle, who liked things just right, to see her belongings being cast about without any rhyme or reason. She was tired and hungry and she didn't want to be anxious on top of that. Besides, she had all the time in the world to organize her new home. She could certainly manage opening one box at a time and placing things were they belonged.

"Look," she said to the sweaty, grumpy men, "just go. I can do this myself."

Without thinking twice, the foreman pushed a clipboard into Rochelle's face for her to sign off on the job, as the other men hopped into their truck eager to drive away, leaving Rochelle standing in a sea of packing paper. But at least it was on her own terms.

She found a box of crackers and some bottled water in a box marked *pantry*, and got to work unpacking.

She labored throughout the night, taking small breaks to rest her aching back, managing to get at least the kitchen unboxed, everything was put into place and it looked beautiful. Surely Harry would be proud of all the work she had done. She laid her hands on her tummy, which grumbled with hunger.

"Oh my God!" Harry's voice, from behind her, startled Rochelle. She didn't realize the time.

"Oh, hi!" She turned to face him, "What do you think? Isn't this kitchen amazing?"

"Amazing? This place looks like a shithole!"

Rochelle's heart sank. "What?" Harry had no clue how hard she had worked, how long it took, just trying to organize her kitchen. Specifically to avoid this exact reaction from him. Nothing ever seemed good enough for him. "Harry...it looks great."

"The rest of the house...there are boxes everywhere!"

"Yes, we are just moving in. Calm down."

"I TOLD you, it was to be a FULL UNPACK!"

"Harry," she tried to reason with her overreactive husband, "the movers were just opening boxes and throwing things everywhere. It was overwhelming, I couldn't handle it."

"I DON'T CARE, ROCHELLE! I PAID for a FULL UNPACK."

"Is this what it's about? Is this about money?" Rochelle felt a pit in her stomach.

"It's about people doing their JOB, Rochelle! Doing what they're TOLD TO DO!"

"Harry, please, I have all the time in the world to organize this house." She felt her throat constrict, a familiar lump, as tears started to form. She thought this move would be good for them—a fresh start.

"I can't trust you to do anything right!"

"Then why weren't YOU here Harry? You have no right to put this all on me, if you couldn't even take the time to help." She cried, wondering why she was even there, in Texas, in their marriage. Her stomach was cramping, she'd had nothing but crackers to eat for twenty-four hours, and her husband was screaming at her about what a failure she was.

"I was WORKING Rochelle!" Harry opened his arms to the room, "Making all THIS possible!"

"I was working too," Rochelle sobbed as she slumped to the floor of her beautiful kitchen. "I want to go home." A kitchen she took all night to unpack—pregnant, hungry and tired, but working anyway, to make it beautiful for her husband. So he would walk in and tell her what a great job she had done, that he was proud of her, for how hard she worked—that he loved her. Instead, he screamed at her, telling her what a failure she was. Rochelle curled into a ball, trying to catch her breath, holding her cramping tummy—something was not right. That evening, she miscarried their baby. She *was* a failure.

Eight-and-a-half years and two deaths later, Rochelle sobbed, on her kitchen floor, scraping Harry's dried blood from in between the cracks of Italian marble. She cursed the floor, the floor that took her baby, the floor that took her husband, as she tried to scrub it free of all its sins.

THE LOUD BANGING on the front door startled Rochelle awake as Moosh barked from inside his crate. Disoriented, she rose from the floor and slowly exited her kitchen, to make her way toward the sound. When did she lie down to fall asleep? As she got closer, she could see an unmistakable silhouette through the textured leaded glass in the front door. Maeve knocked vigorously.

"Honeybee? Roey? Are you in there?" Surely Maeve's knuckles would bruise. "Rochelle? Let me in, honey."

Rochelle took a deep breath and failed at an attempt to smooth her rumpled, slept-in pajamas—she was still wearing the yellow rubber gloves. Removing the gloves, she tossed them on the circular table nestled in the alcove of the foyer, where the buds from Christopher's once spectacular arrangement were now shriveled from thirst, releasing petals in protest. Rochelle pushed her matted hair away from her face with tender hands. She looked down at her palms, pink and blistered from all the scrubbing. Rochelle opened the door for her frantic friend.

"Sweet Baby Jesus! I've been worried sick about you!" Maeve entered like a hurricane, bringing a new and fresh energy into the stagnant space. "Quick, close the door. There are reporters outside."

Rochelle obeyed her friend, peering over Maeve's shoulder to get a glimpse of the few strangers at the curb.

"I've been callin' and callin', sweetie."

"I'm sorry," was all Rochelle could eke out of her dry throat. She hadn't spoken a word to anyone in days.

"Don't you be sorry about a thing," Maeve pulled her friend in close for a hug, and pushed her right back out to examine her. She brushed sandy particles from Rochelle's cheek. "Good God, honeybee, you look awful."

"I'm sorry."

"No, I'm sorry...dang it! I shouldn't have said that."

"Did you say there were reporters outside?"

"Ugh, yes... Nosy Nellies. You know, with everythin' that's happened..."

"Oh," Rochelle could hear Moosh, still barking from his crate, "I've got to let the dog out."

"OK, sweetie, let me help." Maeve followed behind Rochelle, turning lights on in the darkened house as thunder rumbled in the distance. Rochelle looked up to the ceiling and Maeve answered the gesture, "Yep, looks like rains a-comin'."

Rochelle let Moosh out of his crate and he ran through the doggie door to do his business in the yard, quickly returning. Rochelle placed a small plate of food on the floor for him. The usually ravenous pup just sniffed around it, choosing instead to curl up next to Rochelle as she sat in the living room with Maeve.

"Roey, I'm so sorry about Harry. Barrington and I are just sick about it. What can we do for you?"

"I'm OK, Maeve."

"You're obviously not OK." Maeve eyed Rochelle from the top of her frazzled hair down to her bare toes. "When is the last time you ate somethin'? You look so gaunt. That cannot be good for the baby."

"The what?"

"The baby, sweetie," Maeve looked at Rochelle's flat stomach.

Rochelle had forgotten all about her little white lie. The lie she told her husband, in front of his friends, to mess with his head for betraying her trust. "Oh."

"Listen, why don't you hop in the shower and I will make somethin' for you to eat. I'll keep an eye on sweet little Moosh for you."

For the first time in two days, Rochelle realized her stomach ached with hunger. She also knew Maeve would have a lot of questions for her. Twenty more minutes of solitude in a warm shower sounded like a good idea. "OK."

∾

GRATEFUL FOR MAEVE'S VISIT, Rochelle made her way down the windowed hallway toward the master bedroom. It would do her some good to hop into a hot shower and wash away the worries of the past few days, even if only temporarily. Pausing in her bedroom, she opened the wooden window shutters, allowing in the soft muted afternoon light. She picked up her still-charging phone to see fourteen missed calls from Maeve, *sweet friend,* and one from the Dallas police department.

Through the bedroom window, something caught her eye. In the back yard, there was movement on the ground. She slipped the phone into the pocket of her pajama bottoms and opened the French doors leading out to her beautiful garden. Beds bursting with begonia, pretty penta, and globe amaranth welcomed her. This was her happy place. It was the place she found solace and healing, digging in the dirt, being one with the earth. Stepping out onto the flagstone patio, the stones felt warm under her feet, so she slipped into a pair of Harry's rubber slides that had been kicked off by the door. She lifted her face to the sky to feel the warming rays of the sun, but they were nowhere to be found. A gust of wind blew her matted hair, and she opened her eyes to see clouds quickly darkening the once blue summer sky. The rustling breeze and a deep inhale confirmed rain was indeed coming, as she clomped out into the lush grass in the too-big sandals, toward the movement that summoned her.

There, on the ground, in the soft blades of grass, was a young mourning dove, fallen from its nest. *Flutter-flutter, tip-tap.* "Look at you. Poor baby. Where did you come from?" She looked up to a clumsy nest perched on top of the cross beam of the wooden fence surrounding the yard. Some of the nest had become dislodged, most likely by the wind of the impending summer storm. "Ah, little one, you've got to tell your parents to stop building their nests on ledges, when there are plenty of perfectly good branches to protect you." The bird was almost a fledgling but still downy, and not yet old enough to fly as it flittered around on the ground beneath her feet. *I can't let this helpless being lie there.* "Well, we can't just leave you here now, can we? Let's get you somewhere safe."

Rochelle exited her yard, propping the finicky gate open to rustle through her garden shed on the other side of the fence. She gathered a step ladder, a small coconut husk basket liner, a hammer, nail, and a soft towel. Back in her garden, she placed what was left of the original nest into the coconut husk and nailed the husk to the fence, close to its original spot but better protected from the elements. She could hear the melancholy coo of a mature mourning dove, as it watched her from the roof of the house. "Hello, Mama, I'm going to get your baby safely back home." She gingerly picked up the fledgling with the towel, hoping Mama wouldn't swoop down on her, and carefully placed it back into its nest. "There you go, you're safe now. Let's stay in here until you're old enough to fly."

Rochelle closed her ladder and walked back to the shed, turning to see Mama fly back to her baby. She put away the ladder and reached down to pull the prop from the gate; as she looked up, she was startled by a strange round man, standing in her yard, between her and her house.

"Excuse me, Mrs. Hawthorne?" His ruddy face contorted.

"Who's asking?" Rochelle guessed he must have come in through the open gate when she wasn't paying attention.

"Mrs. Hawthorne, I'm Silver Smith, with *The Inquisitor*. It is true you are suspected of the murder of your husband?" He pushed his phone out toward her. Was he recording her?

"Who? What? This is private property! Please leave!" She tried to step around him. But he bobbed his wide girth as she weaved, keeping her in his line of sight.

"We've got word that you yelled from your porch, to your husband, that you were going to kill him."

Doesn't every wife yell that at her husband? "Mr. Smith, please let me pass." Rochelle could hear Moosh barking from inside the house.

"Is it true? Did you tell your husband you were going to kill him?" She heard his phone snap a picture.

Rochelle pulled off Harry's sandals and ran out the gate behind her. The overweight man tried to follow but she slammed the gate in his face, holding her body against it as he spoke through the space in between the wooden boards.

"Mrs. Hawthorne, we have word that you almost ran over a man walking his German shepherd as you fled the scene of the crime."

"Leave me alone!" Rochelle ran around the side of her house, carrying Harry's sandals, and toward the front yard where a small committee reporters were camped out—vultures, waiting for their prey to emerge. Rochelle ducked behind the tall bushes at the front of her house, in just enough time to evade the man, who huffed by. She scooted behind the hedges, hoping to not be seen by the others as she made her way closer to the front door. Daylight was dimming with the now quickly forming clouds and she slipped Harry's sandals back on. The wind blew even stronger, rustling the lush hedges she hid behind. She hoped their parting wouldn't reveal her to the small group of news people. She crouched her tall frame even lower, now squatting in her dead husband's sandals. The breeze blew harder as she sat on the ground, a strong rumble of thunder in the air caused the vultures to hop into their vehicles. *Good, it won't be long now.* A sharp gust of wind and something bopped her on the head.

There, on the ground next to her, lay a cellophane wrapped bundle, delicate flowers, abandoned and brittle, but preserved just the same, in crinkly wrapping, hugged with an ivory bow—a tiny envelope tucked inside. Small drops of rain began to fall as Rochelle opened the envelope and slid out the card embossed with a petite gold heart. The rain pattered a little more, as she recognized the handwriting. The card trembled in her hand as she read. *Sweet Rochelle, I'm so sorry I forgot your birthday. Can you ever forgive me? H-*

Rochelle's tears fell on the ink, diluting Harry's apology into an indigo watercolor. The rain fell even harder, chasing away the vultures. The phone in her pocket rang. Rochelle switched it to silent as quickly as she could. It was Maeve, surely she would be worried. Rochelle texted her.

Maeve...please stay and take care of Moosh. I need some time.

A WALK TO REMEMBER

Rochelle resented every tear falling from her eyes. She resented her soft heart and her kind soul and she resented the fact that she still loved her dead husband. She believed if it weren't for her weak heart, her stupid soul, and her childish love for Harry, she would never have been so foolish as to let herself be deceived by his charade. She would never have let him make her believe that *she* was the one incapable of having a child. She would have pushed for him to be tested, pushed for adoption, pushed for something she so desperately needed in her life. She would have pushed for him to be kind.

Amid all of her resentment there was gratitude. She was grateful for the rain. Grateful that it scared away the vultures waiting for a news story, and grateful that it camouflaged her unwelcome tears as she wandered through the summer storm. Rochelle hugged her arms close to her body, staving off the chill, not knowing if it was from the biting rain raising goosebumps on her flesh, or the memory of Harry.

Why would he do that to her? Why be so cruel as to take away the one thing she desired most, without even giving her a choice? Why didn't Harry want children?

Rochelle needed shelter as the wind forced the rain to needle her

face. She knew of one place, other than her own garden, that would
shelter her body and ease her mind.

THE AUTOMATIC GLASS doors of Rochelle's neighborhood garden
center slid open, and a rush of humid air welcomed her in from the
chilly rain. The condensation on the large windows gave the outside
world an obscure romanticism from inside the warm and balmy refuge.
The center, run by two horticulture PhDs, was always maintained to be
comfortable for the plants, not the people, and Rochelle wouldn't have
it any other way.

Since everyone there knew her, she clomped quickly past the
checkout counters in Harry's large, now-muddy slides, praying not to
be recognized. She worried the clumsy slap of wet sandals against the
concrete floor would draw attention, but it was close to closing time
and the employees seemed to be occupied helping the last few
customers. She made her way past the indoor plants and the quaint bird
feeders, through the potting area stocked with soils, fertilizers, and
colorful clay vessels, around the fragrant flowers and ornamental
grasses, through the shrubs and small trees and into the large greenhouse, which housed edible plants and flowers and the most beautiful
Koi pond Rochelle had ever seen. A few customers ambled around the
front of the store, but no one was near her. Not everyone knew this area
existed, only those who came for weekly gardening classes and
workshops.

Rochelle sat on the teak bench at one side of the Koi pond and let
out a sigh. Hidden behind lemon trees and centered just so, this was the
spot where she could hide and also have the best view of the graceful
orange and black fish swimming among the lily pads. She inhaled the
fresh scent of citrus as she closed her eyes and wiped the rain from her
face with one hand. Her wet pajamas clung to her body and her
stomach growled with a hungry ache—an ache she knew would never
be satisfied. The phone in her pocket buzzed and she opened her eyes,

but she didn't dare look at it, she knew it was Maeve summoning her back. She needed more time.

Rochelle looked down at her clenched right hand, slowly opening it, revealing Harry's crumpled note, now illegible, smudged and smeared from both Rochelle's tears and tight grasp. It didn't matter the words were gone, they were burned into Rochelle's mind. *Forgive me.* How dare Harry ask that of her? Especially when he was asking forgiveness for the wrong sin. There were plenty of times Harry should have asked for forgiveness. He could be a real prick when he was preoccupied. Rochelle remembered another time, a different birthday, when they sat at a small table at one of their favorite restaurants. She didn't want to do anything over the top, just wanted to take a casual Sunday and have a quiet brunch, low key...romantic.

The waiter poured a glass of champagne for both Rochelle and Harry and Rochelle raised her glass, looking forward to Harry's birthday toast, when Harry's phone rang.

"Hold on. I've got to take this."

"Can't it wait just one minute?"

"Rochelle, this is important."

Apparently *she* wasn't. Rochelle waited as long as she could before she drank her warm champagne in a toast to herself.

The buzzing of Rochelle's phone pulled her out of her memory. She was grateful, she hated those memories, learning ways to push them out of her mind. She became an expert at being busy, at finding things to do to occupy her time so she wouldn't have to look at how unhappy she really was. Until now...she never realized.

"Apple?" Rochelle heard a small voice. "It a apple?"

She looked down to see a small child. For a moment, she thought she was hallucinating, dizzy with hunger, her deepest desires manifesting as a mirage. He couldn't have been more than two. He was pointing at the lemon on the tree she sat next to. "It a apple?"

She leaned down toward him. *He is real.* "No, it's a lemon."

"Lemmom!" The child's unruly red hair bounced as he excitedly pronounced the word. Rochelle looked around to see where the child's parents were. Surely they would be near. She saw no one.

"Yes...it's a lemon." Rochelle smiled softly. She noticed his little round belly peeked out of the bottom of his firetruck T-shirt. He had dimpled hands and tiny feet and the biggest brown eyes she'd ever seen. Rochelle suddenly felt sick, overcome with unbearable sadness. Tears filled her eyes, the painful jagged pill stuck in her throat was impossible to swallow.

The child toddled toward Rochelle and her heart began to race. His sweet little hand reached up and took hold of her nervous fingers. "Mama?"

Rochelle gasped. The shock of electricity traveled right through her arm, and pierced her heart. Tears fell from her eyes as she leaned down. She closed her eyes, inhaling deeply, smelling the top of the child's head—sweetness and earth. *Why can't you be mine?* Rochelle saw Heaven in his bespeckled face. *Where is this child's mother? She doesn't deserve him...letting him wander off like this.* Was this her moment? *I can run right now—take him out the back door and disappear and no one would be the wiser. I can pass for his mother. I deserve him.* "We need to find your mama," Rochelle gingerly placed her hand under his dimpled chin, "she is probably worried about you."

"Fwishy!" the toddler squealed, catching sight of the fish in the pond. He neared the water and leaned in to grab.

Rochelle jumped from the bench and took his hand. "Be careful! No water."

"Fwishy!"

"Yes...those are Koi fish."

"Koi fwish!"

Rochelle basked in the moment, until she heard the panicked voice of a woman in the distance. "Rowan!" Rochelle wiped the tears from her face.

"Is your name Rowan?"

"Yes...Rowan!" Rowan pointed both chubby hands at his firetruck T-shirt.

"Well, Rowan, I think your mama is looking for you."

The voice got closer "Rowan!"

"He's in here!" Rochelle called out.

A harried woman and one of the store employees entered the room. Rochelle could see the sheer terror on the woman's face as she ran and knelt in front to her son. "Rowan...oh my God! Don't ever run off like that!" The woman hugged and kissed her son while gently scolding him.

"Fwishy!" Rowan pointed to show his mom.

"Yes, fishy..." The relieved mother laughed and wiped away her own tears. She stood and faced Rochelle, grabbing both her hands. "Thank you so much! I wouldn't know what to do without my child!"

Rochelle's heart hurt. "Of course." Rochelle knew what that felt like.

The woman hugged Rochelle hard and then left with Rowan in hand. Rochelle could still hear him, "Fwishy!" as he disappeared with his thankful mother.

"Mrs. Hawthorne?"

Rochelle had completely forgotten the store employee had entered the room with the distraught mother. The girl looked at Rochelle. Scanned her from her wet matted hair all the way down to her muddy too-big shoes. The girl's open mouth told Rochelle she was mortified by what she saw. Rochelle didn't even try to smooth her appearance, she knew she looked horrifying. She hung her head.

"Mrs. Hawthorne, are you OK? I'm...I'm so sorry about Mr. Hawthorne." Did Rochelle see pity on the girl's face? "We're about to close and...well...I'm...I'm going to have to ask you to leave."

"Oh...of...of course, I'm so sorry. Of course."

Rochelle quickly exited the greenhouse, leaving behind the edible flowers and plants and the graceful Koi. She, again, passed the ornamental grasses and fragrant flowers, walked around the colorful clay vessels in the potting area with its bagged dirt and fertilizers, and through the indoor plants and quaint bird feeders, all the way to the front of the store and past the checkout counters where the remaining employees were all standing—in silence, watching the ghost of a woman they once knew ashamedly clomp out of her local garden center.

16

REMEMBERING WHAT'S IMPORTANT

ain drummed atop the canopy of the now-closed garden center as Rochelle accepted its shelter from the storm, huddled under it, in the dark of night. The buzzing phone in her pocket could not be ignored, and she pulled it out of her damp pajama bottoms. There were multiple texts from Maeve.

Where are you?

Roey?

Girl, when are you coming home?

Still here...waiting for your reply.

Tried to feed Moosh, he seems depressed.

Seriously, just text me back so I don't have to worry about you.

The po-po stopped by...something about a video? Says he'll be by tomorrow.

Hey...Moosh looks kind of lethargic.

Rochelle...I think something's seriously wrong with Moosh. He's vomit-

Rochelle panicked as her phone battery died. What was Maeve trying to tell her? She clicked buttons in desperation, trying, unsuccessfully, to bring the darkened screen back to life. She needed to get home to Moosh. Why had she been feeling so sorry for herself, fantasizing about a child when she had the best little buddy living right under her own roof? She didn't know what she'd do if anything were to happen to him. She needed a ride, and needed it now. Seeing a car leaving the parking lot, she guessed it was one of the garden center employees. She waved her arms wildly, trying to flag it down. "Hey! Hey!"

The car slowed and the window opened. She didn't recognize the driver, who took one look at her disheveled mess and yelled, "Get a job, you bum!" before speeding off.

17

FAKE NEWS

Rochelle sat in her living room and gingerly submerged one bruised and battered foot at a time into a tub of warm water mixed with Epsom salts and a few drops of eucalyptus oil. Not able to flag a ride the night before, she was forced to remove Harry's sandals and run barefoot, all the way home, to get to her ailing Moosh.

"Sweet Jesus!" Maeve exclaimed when a wet and panting Rochelle burst through the door.

"Where's Moosh?" Rochelle tossed Harry's useless sandals aside.

"In his kennel, honeybee."

Rochelle ran to the kennel where Moosh lay curled up, motionless. He barely lifted his head when Rochelle reached in to grab him.

"What's wrong, baby?" She lifted him to her chest.

"He ate just a little bit, but then he started to vomit a short while later." Maeve chewed on the inside of her lip. "Then he looked like he was trying to do his business outside, but it was watery."

"OK," Rochelle hugged her little buddy close, "let's get him to the vet."

Now, swishing her feet in the soothing water, she awaited the call from Dr. Herzog, whose staff persuaded Rochelle to leave Moosh overnight for observation. They assured her he was in good hands, they would give him fluids and do a full workup—that *she* looked as if she needed to go home to rest and they would call her in the morning. She turned on the television and switched it to mute.

Rochelle closed her eyes and said a silent prayer, asking that Moosh would be OK. She promised God that she would not take anything else for granted if he'd do her that one favor. She would move forward with her life and not look back in regret or resentment. As she opened her eyes, she regretted and resented what she saw.

On her muted television were two familiar faces. One with beige hair, donning coke-bottle glasses, and the other with black lipstick and raven hair to match. Rochelle turned up the volume to see Earl and the checkout girl from McCreedy's General being interviewed on local Fox news by a bouffant blonde.

"...and can you tell me your impression of the woman when she visited your store?"

"She was a real fancy lookin' lady." Earl pushed his glasses up the bridge of his nose, distorting his eyes even more, "I didn't think a lady like that would 'preciate gittin' dirty."

"So you believe she wasn't really buying those gardening supplies to garden?"

"Well...let's see...she had that there shovel in her hands...and that there lye in her cart...and I was askin' her if she was to be amendin' her soil..."

"For Pete's sake, Earl!" the checkout girl elbowed Earl out of the way, putting herself between Earl and the interviewer. "By the time you finish, I'll be needin' my roots dyed!" The bossy girl positioned her lanky self in front of the camera and adjusted her holey tee, pushing her nonexistent breasts upward, failing at better cleavage. "The name's Liberty," she chomped on her gum and smiled into the camera as the reporter tried to follow her mouth with the microphone, "and I remember that lady. She was definitely plannin' on murderin' someone, hidin' behind those big designer sunglasses."

Bouffant corrected her. "Thank you, Liberty, but for the record, wearing sunglasses doesn't necessarily make one a murderer."

"Yeah, but the lye in her cart does."

Earl tried to step in, "Well...not if she was amendin' the soil..."

"Back off, Earl," Liberty, held her arm across Earl's chest and looked melodramatically into the camera, which slowly zoomed in. "You see..." She removed the gum from her mouth and stuck it to the back of her hand. "...I could tell she was thinkin' reeeal bad thoughts. The way she was holdin' on to that shoppin' cart with both hands, white knuckles and all. She hardly looked me in the eye once I spotted the lye...and then...the way she suspiciously swiped that credit card..."

"Wait a minute," bouffant interrupted and the camera panned out, "she used a credit card? Why would a person planning on doing something bad use a credit card and not cash?"

Liberty grimaced at the interviewer, clearly offended for being interrupted. "Uh! As I was say-in'..." the camera slowly zoomed back in, "...the way she swiped that credit card—it was a fast swipe, like she had somewhere to be. Like at a murder. And then...she took off runnin' like a guilty woman! Even left her shovel behind!"

The camera zoomed out to reveal Earl, holding up Rochelle's forgotten shovel and smiling. "An' you can git one just like this at McCreedy's General! Mention the word *murder* for ten percent off yer purchase!"

"Restrictions apply!" Liberty added with a wink, popping her gum back in her mouth and chewing through her smile.

The camera cut to bouffant, mouth hanging open, speechless. Rochelle's phone rang—it was the veterinarian's office. She clicked off the television.

"Hello?"

"Mrs. Hawthorne?"

"Yes, Dr. Herzog, how's Moosh?"

"Well, our X-rays show he has an acute gastrointestinal obstruction."

"A what?" Rochelle pulled on her bottom lip.

"A blockage...in his intestines."

"Oh no, what would cause that?"

"He's definitely ingested something foreign, a piece of metal. I can't tell exactly what it is from the X-rays. We'll know once we remove it. I'd like to operate immediately, if I have your permission."

"Uh...yes, of course!" Rochelle was dumbfounded, "Metal? Should I come in to the office?"

"No, it would do you best to stay home, there's nothing you can do here. I'll call you to let you know when we are finished."

"OK, Doctor, but..."

"We'll take good care of him, Mrs. Hawthorne."

"OK, thank you."

"Talk soon."

The line went dead and Rochelle sank deeper into her sofa, thinking of Moosh as she tried to find comfort in the warmth surrounding her aching feet.

18

DETECTIVE WHAT'S-HIS-NAME

Rochelle woke to the sound of the doorbell. It took a minute for her to realize where she was, her feet still submerged in a now chilly tub of water. She stepped onto the towel on the floor and quickly dried her feet before opening the door for Detective Blankenship.

"Mrs. Hawthorne." The detective stood, holding on to the brim of his hat, as he tipped his head to Rochelle. Behind him, the rain continued to pour from the day before. Rochelle peered over the officer's shoulder and was surprised to see the vultures were still out front, now huddled under an unstably erected canopy; her trampled front yard bore waterlogged, muddy footprints from the inconsiderate reporters.

"Hi, Detective, come on in from the rain."

The officer took off his cap and shook the raindrops onto the porch as he thumbed backward. "How long have they been out there?"

"Ever since..." Rochelle didn't need to explain as the officer stepped inside, "they're trying to get a view of the murderess."

"Ah, I'm sorry about that. When I leave, I'll tell them there's no story here. I stopped by to let you know you've been officially cleared of suspicion. The time stamp on your credit card receipt plus the witnesses from McCreedy's place you there at the time of the assault. Everything checks out."

The news didn't make Rochelle feel much better. "Thanks for letting me know. I wish you'd deliver the message to McCreedy's General."

"Ma'am?"

"Never mind. Come inside." The detective followed Rochelle into her kitchen and she ushered him into a seat at the table. "Do you have any leads on any suspects?"

The detective sat. "Not yet. There were no unusual prints taken from the scene and without any witnesses or a murder weapon, it's going to take some time. But we'll get to the bottom of it."

"Can I offer you anything? Coffee? Water? Iced tea?"

"No, thanks. Did you and your husband have any other surveillance cameras? Other than the one outside your husband's office door?"

"Oh, I forgot about that camera." Rochelle sat and lifted one leg, resting her foot on the opposite knee and began to rub her sole. "No, we don't have any others. Did you see something on the footage from that camera?"

"Nothing that can help us. Just your husband and delivery people. The same thing you probably saw when you checked the footage." The officer watched as she kneaded her foot, "There was nothing suspicious the day of the murder."

"Oh. I never checked that camera. Harry was the only one who ever did. He had it installed outside his office door, specifically for deliveries. A while back our neighborhood had a rash of someone stealing packages and large envelopes. He has..." Rochelle looked down, not used to speaking of Harry in past tense, "*had,* a lot of important documents and equipment delivered here, for his business, and since it was on the other side of the house, he wanted to be able to keep an eye on it when he wasn't in his office." Rochelle placed her foot on the ground and lifted the opposite leg, massaging her other foot.

"So, you never monitored it?"

"Never really needed to."

"You OK?" The detective nodded toward her feet.

"Uhm," Rochelle stopped massaging her foot, "yes, I'm fine...long story."

The officer continued, "I saw that side of the house does have a coded gate."

"Yes, but people are clever. They learn how to get around the system."

"Understood. Which brings us back to the video...there was nothing suspicious around the time of the murder, but on a few past occasions, the camera was moved."

"What do you mean moved?" Rochelle placed her foot on the ground to meet the other and sat up in her chair. "You sure I can't get you something?"

"Actually, coffee would be nice," the detective removed his hat and placed it on the table, "...the camera was turned upwards, toward the sky."

Rochelle rose and quickly washed her hands, then approached the gourmet Bosch coffee unit built into the kitchen wall. Walking around the large island, she carefully stepped over the area on the floor with the thin brown grout lines. She placed a mug under the double spout. "Coffee or espresso? Why would someone turn the camera to the sky?"

"Just regular coffee, please...ya got me...I have no idea why."

Rochelle turned a dial and pressed a button, and the unit began to grind unseen coffee beans. "Milk?"

"Black."

"Can you see who it was? See who turned the camera?" Steamy hot coffee magically filled the mug.

"I believe it was your husband."

Rochelle felt someone touch her shoulder; she turned to see the detective sitting at the table looking at his cell phone and a chill ran down her spine. The machine spit steam, signaling it was done. Rochelle took the mug from the maker and walked around the opposite side of the island, avoiding the thin brown grout lines, before she placed the mug in front of the detective.

"Would I be able to take a look at that footage?"

"You own the software, ma'am. You can just log in."

"Oh, right, I will then." Rochelle nodded and pursed her lips, chewing the inside of her mouth as she stared at the thin brown grout lines behind the detective.

The detective sipped, "This is great, thanks. If you spot anything of interest, anything I might have missed, please let me know."

"I will." Rochelle couldn't take her eyes off the floor. She wondered why he couldn't see it. Rochelle studied the detective for the next twenty minutes, waiting for him to notice. Nothing.

"Well, that's all I have." Detective Blankenship stood twenty minutes later and offered his hand, "If there's anything else, please let me know."

"Thank you." Rochelle walked with him and opened the door. "Detective?"

"Ma'am."

She studied his face for a bit, "Never mind."

THUNDER SHOOK THE HOUSE, and Rochelle immediately worried about Moosh. She dialed the veterinarian's office, but when they answered, they quickly put her on hold. She needed to make sure they were taking care of him. Did they know he was afraid of thunder? Who was going to soothe him during the storm? She held the phone between the crick of her neck and her shoulder, listening to Barry Manilow as she sat at her dining room table, typing away on Harry's laptop, trying to remember which password she needed to get into it. She wanted to see the surveillance footage herself.

Why didn't she know his password? Did she actually ever know it? She never needed nor wanted to log in to her husband's computer. She wasn't the type of wife that was going to check up on her husband. Unfortunately, in hindsight, it seemed Harry was the type of husband she *should* have checked up on. What other pink skeletons were hiding in his closet?

"Hello, thank you for holding," Blue-hair interrupted Rochelle's train of thought.

"Oh, hi!" Rochelle grabbed the phone and stood. "This is Rochelle Hawthorne, I was calling, well, because it's thundering and Moosh is afraid…he is afraid of the thunder."

"Well, aren't you a sweetie," Blue-hair lilted on the other end, "don't you worry about your little guy, he is actually in surgery right now and he won't be able to hear a thing."

"He is?" Rochelle's heart broke a little imaging his small body as an anesthetized tiny lump of fur.

"Yes, he'll be just fine. I'm sure the storm will be gone by the time he wakes up. This is Texas, it can't rain that much longer."

"OK, well…when he does wake up and if it's still thundering, will you please put a weighted blanket over him? That always soothes him."

"Yes, sweetie, we will. I'll make a note of it on his chart."

"Thank you."

Rochelle hung up and looked at Harry's laptop, with its generic picture of a deserted beach filling the screen. In the middle was an empty rectangular box, taunting her, daring her to guess the magic combination of letters, numbers, and characters that would allow her passage.

A flash of lightening and a rumble of thunder made her think of Moosh, made her think of what was important, and she slapped the laptop closed.

19

DINNER WITH ROCHELLE

T he tinkling of sterling flatware against delicate porcelain pulled Rochelle's soft focus back into the dimmed dining room. Her head felt under water, ears muffled, as she sat at the long table, surrounded by friends, who were engaged in somewhat subdued conversations. Her mind had been elsewhere, worrying about Moosh and the call she'd had earlier with Dr. Herzog.

"Hello, Mrs. Hawthorne?"

"Yes, hello, Doctor," Rochelle was standing in her pantry, focused on the jarred spices as she arranged them into alphabetical order.

"Well, the operation was a success."

"Ah, thank God!" She clasped the tarragon to her chest.

"But...we are not out of the woods yet."

"Why? What does that mean?" *Tarragon. T.*

"His vitals are a bit unstable, he was under sedation for a long time."

"But, he's going to be OK, right, Doctor?" *T, T, T.*

"We'll need to keep him overnight for observation."

"And then? He will be fine?"

"We'll do our best, Mrs. Hawthorne. Call you tomorrow."

"Don't forget, he's afraid of the thun—"

The doctor hung up and Rochelle stood, staring at the jar of tarragon for a long while, willing her mind away from negative thoughts about Moosh. She *needed* him to be OK, he was her whole life. *T, T, T*...she placed the tarragon in between the cayenne and cinnamon and closed the door. Being alone in the house without Moosh was unthinkable. Being alone with her anxious thoughts would be unbearable.

An anxious Rochelle called Maeve and asked if she would bring dinner

MAEVE BROUGHT DINNER, Barrington, Christopher, and Mirabelle. She also brought a sedative for Rochelle—something to take the edge off.

"Eat, honeybee," Maeve spooned what looked to be undercooked meatloaf mixed with noodles from a casserole dish onto the hand-painted plate.

"I'm not that hungry." Rochelle scrutinized the colorless food.

"When is the last time you had an actual meal?"

"What day is it again?"

"It's Wednesday night, honey," Maeve slid Rochelle's plate closer.

"Oh shit," Mirabelle pulled out her phone and started pressing buttons, "the girls have SAT practice in the morning."

Barrington snickered, forking anemic noodles into his mouth.

"What's so funny about that?" Mirabelle peered over her phone at Barrington.

Rochelle pushed unappetizing food around her plate. "Gee...I thought it was still Tuesday."

"Could be the opioids my wife gave you," Barrington chaffed.

Maeve frowned at her husband. "Shhh! She was anxious."

"Opioids?" Mirabelle put her phone away and poured herself a glass of wine.

"We're all anxious." Christopher croaked as Mirabelle refilled his wine glass.

Rochelle watched Christopher lift his glasses and dab his swollen eyes with his napkin. "Are you OK?" she asked.

"No, I'm not OK. I don't know how you can stay in this house, Rochelle."

Neither can I. "This is my home. Where would you like me to go?"

Silence lingered, interrupted by the sound of Barrington's chewing, drawing the eyes of his friends. He looked up from his plate and stopped. "What?"

Christopher pushed away from the table, "Ugh, I need a minute," and left the room.

Mirabelle apologized for her friend, "He's been on edge ever since..." She stopped herself.

"It's OK," said Rochelle, "like Chris said, we are all anxious."

"So! I heard you're taking the girls to China, Mirabelle?" Maeve changed the subject.

"Yes...in a few days..."

Rochelle rose from the table, "Can you excuse me for a moment? I'm going to make a cup of coffee."

Rochelle tried to shake the fog from her head as she entered the kitchen. Whatever Maeve gave her, a pill from her own prescription, was too strong a dose for Rochelle's thin frame. Rochelle opened the tall door to the walk-in pantry and stepped inside, mindlessly scanning the shelves, forgetting why she was there in the first place. After a few unsuccessful minutes of trying to remember, she spotted the tarragon in the wrong place. She lifted the glass container and placed it in between the seasoned salt and thyme, letting out a satisfied breath. She stepped out and closed the door, startled by movement on the kitchen floor. "Christopher?"

"Oh! Oh, Rochelle," Christopher was on all fours in the kitchen.

"What are you doing down there?" *Is it the thin brown lines?*

He rose from the floor, brushing off his knees, "I...I didn't see you. I was looking for my contact lens."

"Oh," She blinked softly, slowly, not quite registering the eyeglasses on his face, "I hope you find it."

"Thanks..." After an awkward pause, Christopher grabbed

Rochelle by the shoulders and pulled her close as he sobbed. "Oh Rochelle, I'm so sorry about Harry. It's just awful. If you need anything, please don't hesitate to ask."

Rochelle hugged Christopher—apathetic and anesthetized, her emotions as bland as the noodles on her abandoned plate. "Thank you." Rochelle could have stayed propped on Christopher longer if it weren't for the commotion summoning them back into the dining room.

"Why do you have to be such an arrogant prick?" Mirabelle shot at Barrington. Heated, she removed the silk scarf from around her neck and placed it on the back of her chair.

"I'm just saying," Barrington continued, "I don't understand why you have to put your twins through so much rigamarole. Don't you think they're over-scheduled? They have plenty of time to prepare for college. Take it easy. When they get older they will either get in to Harvard or they won't."

"That's easy for you to say, your boys are already there," adding with a mumble, *"God knows how."*

"I heard that, and what's that supposed to mean, anyway?" Barrington puffed his chest.

"C'mon Barrington, you know your boys aren't the sharpest tools in the shed. If it weren't for rowing, they wouldn't be at Harvard."

"That, and a sizable donation," Christopher chimed from the doorway.

"Now come on y'all, that isn't very nice to say about the boys," Maeve defended Barrington's children, products of his first marriage.

Mirabelle softly turned to Maeve. "Maeve, if those boys were biologically yours, they'd be smart as a whip. Unfortunately, they're not."

Maeve didn't disagree. "Your girls are smart cookies, Mirabelle. Just like their mama. They'll be just fine."

"It's not only being smart, Maeve, Harvard has a reputation for being biased against Asian Americans."

"Bullshit!" Barrington protested.

"It's true! They hold us to a higher standard. Although we rate better academically and extracurricularly, they penalize us when it comes to the personal assessments, because we are deemed *too quiet* to be valuable additions to the student body."

Barrington snorted, "I hate to enlighten you, Mirabelle, but you broke the mold on the Asians-being-quiet thing."

Unamused, Mirabelle stood from the table. "Ugh, that's it...I've got to go. I'm fucking exhausted and I have to be up early with the girls." She walked over to Rochelle, who was still standing in the door-way, leaning on Christopher. Mirabelle squeezed Rochelle tight. "Hang in there, babe. Call me if you need anything."

"I will..." Rochelle needed coffee, suddenly remembering why she wandered into the kitchen earlier. "Listen, everyone, thank you all for being here. It's getting late, and we're all emotional and tired. You've done so much, you don't have to stay with me any longer. I think I'll be fine now. I think I need some time alone."

"Are you sure, honeybee? What about this mess?" Maeve gestured at the table of half the eaten food, cheap noodles on expensive china. Unfortunately, the prettiest table setting couldn't redeem the unappe-tizing food.

"I'll take care of it, it'll give me something to do...keep my mind off things."

After the last of her friends left, Rochelle dialed a number on her phone. "Hello? Yes, I'd like to speak to someone about replacing the floor in my kitchen. Yes, I'll hold..."

THE SWIRLING STEAM from the hot coffee felt good on Rochelle's face, as she sat in the dark at one end of her dining room table, her thoughts inexhaustible. She took in a deep breath and assessed the work ahead. At the other end of the table, half-eaten plates of food and half-drunk glasses of wine laid scattered and abandoned—remnants of friends. She could almost see their ghosts, sitting at their places, engaged in voiceless conversation. Some laughing with shared stories, leaning in toward each other, smiling in blissful harmony. Others battling competitively, faces growling, while throwing silent insults at each other, arms and hands animating every word. Rochelle was happy her friends came to spend time with her, to take her mind off of things. She was also relieved when they left.

The dining room needed to be her new home base. She wasn't able to spend more than ten minutes alone in her kitchen—not since finding Harry, not since the thin brown lines. When Moosh was with her, he was a buffer and it was bearable. But alone, she felt Harry's presence weighing heavily on her shoulders.

Her hands cradled her favorite mug, white on the outside, embossed with the words *OH SHIT,* coffee stained on the inside from years of overuse. It was a free gift, a promo from her local garden center when she bought five bags of fertilizer for a new flower bed. Harry hated that mug, said it was cheap and classless. She inhaled the coffee's steamy arabica aroma, letting its warmth flow deep into her lungs. She hoped it, and the previous cup she drank, would curtail her brain fog—dissipate the effects of Maeve's horse pill. She was through with self-medicating, it made her feel useless, less than.

Less than—it was how Harry made her feel with his continual criticism of the way she did things. She didn't fold the towels tight enough or didn't iron his shirts crisp enough. The filet mignon was a little overdone and the salmon a little under. For all her efforts, she certainly didn't polish the sterling flatware to the precise shine, and when she was through hand-washing the heirloom porcelain, she'd forgotten to place a tissue between each plate, endangering the hand-painted embellishments and platinum rims. Now they were less valuable. Now *she* was less valuable. *Oh, and the dead baby...*

Rochelle sipped from her free mug, pushing the tablecloth away at her end and gingerly settling the mug back down on the bare tabletop, being careful not to chip its base. Her eyes fell on each and every extravagant and overpriced serving piece left abandoned at the opposite end of the dining room table. Rising from her chair, she lifted the rubber trash bin she'd taken from the kitchen built-in and walked it to the other end of the table. She leaned over the table with her body, stretching out her arm to span its shortest width. With one smooth swipe of her arm, she pushed all the priceless place settings into the garbage bin. Expensive porcelain plates with hand-painted embellishments and platinum, smeared with cold cheap noodles, crashed into the bin. Waterford crystal stemware, their rims clouded with faint lipstick kisses, toppled over, spilling red wine onto the white silk tablecloth and into the waiting rubber receptacle. She held no bias as she swiped monogrammed flatware, fabric napkins, and sterling salt and pepper shakers onto the pile of discarded treasures.

She didn't stop until she'd swiped it all—*all* of the heirlooms, the judgment, the criticism, the lies. For heirlooms aren't always made of porcelain, or sterling, or crystal. Some heirlooms are the bad habits handed down to us by our ancestors, the things we refuse to change about ourselves because we either cannot recognize them in ourselves or we don't want to do the work to change them. Rochelle swiped until she shattered all of the things Harry brought into their marriage. All of the things—both physical, and learned.

All but her priceless free mug, which she loved, as she sat back down and carefully raised it to her mouth, sipping, reassessing what she deemed valuable.

20

APOLOGIES

"HELLO?" Rochelle barked into her phone, trying to speak over the earsplitting noise coming from her kitchen. She couldn't quite make out the muffled voice on the other line, "HANG ON A SEC," and moved into her bedroom where it was quiet.

"Rochelle?"

"Yes...oh...hi, Mirabelle."

"Where the hell are you?"

"I'm at home."

"What the hell is that wretched noise?"

"Oh, I'm having the kitchen floor replaced."

"What? Why?"

The thin brown grout lines. "I'm ready for a change."

"Oh." Mirabelle seemed to disappear.

"Mir?"

"Yes, sorry, I just wanted to call to say I'm so sorry about the argument last night."

"It's not a problem, Mir. There's no need to apologize. Since Harry...since Harry died, everyone's been on edge." Rochelle traced her mug's embossed words with her finger. Her morning coffee was almost gone, only the remnants of frothed cream remained, clinging to the inner walls of the stained mug, like stratus clouds in an amber sky. "I'm sorry I was such a zombie. Whatever Maeve gave me was strong as hell."

"Pshaw...don't you apologize for anything. You'd better be careful what you take though...in your condition. Who knows what that was? Probably some fucking leftover from one of her surgeries?"

"In my condition? Oh..." *Dammit, I keep forgetting.* "Yes, who knows?"

"Plus, Barrington probably likes to keep her medicated so she won't discover what a troll he is." Mirabelle's voice muffled, "Girls, don't forget to pack your music books...I'll meet you in the car!"

"What's *with* you two lately? You and Barrington?"

"Honestly, I don't know. He just pushes my fucking buttons. He's such an arrogant asshole. Which reminds me, I left my scarf hanging on the chair last night."

"Oh yes, it's still there."

"Good, would you mind if I stopped by later this afternoon to pick it up? I'd like to bring it with me on the trip."

"Sure...Could we make it another day, though, I'm waiting for the call to pick up Moosh."

"OK...that works... Lily...Ivy...in the car!"

"When do you leave, Mir?"

"In a little over a week...I can't believe the girls haven't seen Chao in months. His parents can't wait to get their hands on them, instill some Chinese culture—think they are becoming too Americanized."

"You mean they are going to undo everything their Uncle Christopher has taught them?" Rochelle chuckled.

Mirabelle laughed, "Haha, yes! All that sugar daddy shit."

"What's he going to do for a month without you, Mir?"

"Oh my God, Rochelle, he's been such a mess lately. Having a hard time keeping it together. Maybe you can keep an eye on him when I'm gone?"

"I'll make sure to spend time with him. Oh...by the way, if you talk to him today, tell him I swept the floor before the workers arrived, but I couldn't find his contact lens."

"His what?"

"His contact lens? He was on the floor looking for it last night."

"Huh!" Mirabelle paused, then, "He doesn't wear contact lenses."

"He doesn't?"

"No...he's so severely nearsighted, they don't make a strength that works for him."

"Oh," Rochelle was confused, "maybe I was mistaken, I *was* a bit loopy." Rochelle's phone beeped, it was the Animal Hospital calling. "Oh! Gotta go!"

She clicked off before Mirabelle had a chance to say goodbye.

"Hello?"

"Mrs. Hawthorne?"

"Yes."

"Moosh is ready for you!"

"Great! Be right there!"

WHITE LIES

Maeve pulled the small white paper from the front pocket of Barrington's suit pants and placed it on the counter. She bundled the pants and the rest of the clothing into the nylon bag, pulled the draw string, and hung the bag on the hook on the front porch, ready for the dry cleaning service to pick it up.

BARRINGTON RUMMAGED THROUGH HIS CLOSET, turning all the linings of his suit pants inside out.

"What are you looking for?" Maeve called from the bathroom mirror as she applied a second coat of mascara to her lashes.

"Nothing."

MAEVE UNFOLDED the small white paper. The scribbled phone number was unfamiliar to her, as was the handwriting. She trusted her husband. She dialed the number anyway. After the second ring a woman answered. Maeve hung up.

DISTRACTIONS

C hristopher stood in front of the three-way mirror, in the private dressing room of the Gucci store, surveying how his ass fit into the snug windowpane plaid pants. "Does this plaid make my ass look fat?"

"No…your ass makes your ass look fat!" Mirabelle wore a chic, black tailored suit with a leopard print pussy bow blouse as she sat in a royal blue, overstuffed, gilded Baroque chair, sipping on rosé.

Christopher alternated hands in front of himself—one held a vest with an elaborate floral print, the other, an intricate bird print. "Flowers or birds? I can't decide."

"Elephants."

He held up a pleasantly gaudy tie, "What about this tie?"

"Christopher! Are you even listening to me?"

"Mir, what? Oh my God! I'll take them all!" He threw the lot to the salivating saleswoman who silently stood off to the side, quickly gathering the pieces of clothing, "Put them on my account." He pulled off the pants and tossed those to her as well, right before she scampered off. Christopher sat himself into a matching chair, in his underwear and dress shirt, and began to sample the cheeses arranged into flowers on the small silver platter that sat on the table in between them. "Have you tried this Gruyere?"

"What the fuck is wrong with you? You've been so distracted. Tell me what's going on in your head." Mirabelle refilled her rosé. "And make it quick, because I have to pick the girls up from piano in…" she tapped her phone screen, "in ninety minutes."

"What do you mean, distracted?" He smeared some brie on a cracker.

"I mean…you are distracted, and emotional, and overspending," she widened her eyes, "and soon to be overeating—to compensate for something. What is it?"

Christopher chomped on the cheesy cracker and pushed his glasses up the bridge of his nose. His right leg bounced up and down with nervous energy.

"Mir…can I tell you something?"

"Christopher, I am *asking* you to tell me something."

"I mean, can I tell you something and you won't get mad at me?" He placed a second cracker with schmear back onto the platter.

"I'm not going to get mad."

"Maybe I should put my pants on first?"

"Oh…my…God…"

"OK, never mind," he nervously rubbed the velour upholstery on the chair's arms, "Harry told me something, a few weeks before he died."

"He did? What did he tell you?"

"It's about Barrington." His fingers continued excoriating the plush.

"Is that bastard having an affair behind Maeve's back?"

"Not sure, but there's something worse than that…well, *you'll* think it's worse."

Mirabelle held her slender pointer finger in the air, long red nail a warning flag, "Wait a minute, before you tell me anything, do you think this could have something to do with what happened to Harry?"

"It could…possibly…"

Mirabelle inhaled deeply and sat up straight, closing her eyes like a Zen bodhisattva in a tailored Tom Ford suit, "What then?"

Christopher looked around the private dressing room, making sure no other ears were listening. He leaned in close to Mirabelle, cupping either side of his mouth before whispering into her ear.

Mirabelle's scream summoned the terrified saleswoman, who burst into the dressing room as rosé dripped down the three-way mirror.

23

FINDING TREASURE

R ochelle hugged Moosh ever so delicately as he sat in her lap while she waited in the small room of the animal hospital, being careful not to press on the pup's new stitches. She couldn't stop poking her face into his cone and kissing the top of his woozy head, as the doctor recited his discharge instructions.

"Now remember," Dr. Herzog continued, "you'll need to monitor his wound for redness and swelling, and call us if anything seems out of the ordinary. Can you do that?"

"Of course I can." She kissed Moosh again. He smelled of antiseptic.

"You'll also need to restrict his activity at home. He'll be groggy for the first day or so but will perk up soon after that."

"Will do." Moosh's warmth calmed Rochelle's soul.

"He'll have regained his appetite. Make sure you feed him a bland diet for the first few days. There's a list of acceptable foods printed on a sheet in the packet the girls will give you when checking out. Gradually, you can return him to a normal diet."

"Speaking of eating," Rochelle was glad she remembered, "is there any way to slow him down? He scarfs down his food so quickly."

"Yes, ask the girls up front. There are a few bowls on the market that can help you with that."

"OK, sounds simple enough." Rochelle stood, she couldn't wait to get back home to snuggle with her pup.

"Oh, I almost forgot." The doctor pulled a small clear bag from behind the counter and handed it to Rochelle. She took the bag from him with one hand, cradling Moosh with the other. "Here's the ring he ingested."

"The ring?" Rochelle peered through the plastic but didn't recognize the thin band. She'd get a better look at it when she was home and her hands were free. "That's so odd."

"Indeed, you're very lucky. The way it was embedded, because there is a hole in the middle, it did not obstruct his bowel completely, and most likely saved his life."

Rochelle's eyes moistened, "Oh my gosh, Doctor, thank you so much for taking care of him." She kissed Moosh again.

"My pleasure, Mrs. Hawthorne, you do the same."

"I will."

24

CONVERSATIONS

Maeve heard a muffled Barrington from the other room, having a hushed argument with whoever was on the phone. The slam of something, and then a moment of silence, was her clue she was free to enter his office. Maeve peeked her head through the heavy door. "What's goin' on in here, baby?"

"Nothing," Barrington snapped his laptop closed.

"You sure were arguin' with a whole lotta nothin'." Maeve entered and made her way behind the desk, sitting on her husband's lap, causing the squeaky rolling chair to lean back on its hinges. "You sure you don't want to tell me what's botherin' you, sweetie?" She brushed back his white hair and kissed his forehead, detecting the salt in the light perspiration above his brow.

"Not now, Maeve," Barrington let out a burdened sigh.

"Are you sure?" She kissed his forehead again, followed with little pecks, making her way toward his ear.

Barrington placed both his hands on his wife's waist, "Mm-hmm," and lifted her up from her sitting position until she was standing again. "I can't right now."

Maeve couldn't remember a time when her husband ever spurned her advances. "Well, that's a first." She walked away, toward the door.

Barrington threw his hands up. "What do you want, Maeve?"

She turned at the door, "I want you to tell me what's wrong with you. You've been so irritable lately."

"There's nothing wrong with me!" Barrington picked up his fountain pen and popped off the cap, immediately snapping it back on again.

"Why are you so fidgety?"

"I'm not fidgety." He continued to snap the pen's cap on and off.

Maeve, hands on hips, stared at the pen, "You're not?"

Barrington threw the pen onto his desk, "Dammit pumpkin, I don't want to talk about it right now."

"Talk about what?" she needled.

"What do you want me to say, Maeve?"

"Tell me what's happenin'. Who were you yellin' at? Why did you slam your computer closed like you've got somethin' to hide?"

Barrington didn't answer his wife, just chewed on the inside of his cheek, elbows on the desk, head in his hands.

"Are you havin' an affair?"

Barrington shook his head, still in his hands. Maeve slammed the door as she left. She didn't believe him.

25

REVELATIONS

Rochelle left her car parked in the driveway—exactly where she wanted—and entered her house with a groggy Moosh in her arms. It was quiet. There was no jackhammer noise coming from the kitchen, nor Tejano music blaring from a transistor radio. There was nothing but silence. Rochelle gave the workers the day off so Moosh could rest. Nothing was going to interfere with his recovery. She peeked into the kitchen, where the floor was completely torn up, where marble shards were piled in mounds, ready to be hauled off. Most importantly, there were no more thin grout lines haunting her.

She settled Moosh on the floor in front of his water bowl in the dining room, she filled the bowl with bottled water. The pup's cone completely covered the bowl and his head seemed to disappear as he drank. Laps of water echoed within the conical plastic walls, making Rochelle giggle as she dialed Detective Blankenship.

"Blankenship."

"Hello, Detective? It's Rochelle Hawthorne."

"Hi, Mrs. Hawthorne, you sound in good spirits."

"Yes, my dog is amusing me, getting used to his recovery collar."

"Did he have an operation? Hope it wasn't too serious."

"He's doing fine now, ate something he shouldn't have. They

removed the blockage." Rochelle placed the clear bag containing the ring onto her dining room table, along with the packet of post-op instructions the receptionist had given her. She followed Moosh around the house as he navigated in his new accessory. "I was wondering if I could take a look at the footage from the surveillance camera? I can't seem to log on to Harry's computer to get to the app."

"Sure, I can email you the link we received from the security company. It will have the complete history, probably more than you would find on his computer anyway."

Rochelle watched Moosh trot out of the dining room and across the dusty subfloor in the kitchen, bumping into his doggie door, the cone prohibiting his passage, the pup confused as to why he couldn't exit. "OK, that would be great." She followed her pup.

"Let me know if anything looks out of the ordinary to you. Anything to help us find your husband's murderer."

Harry's murderer—why hadn't it dawned on her before? Her husband was stabbed, in his own home, in *her* home. And it wasn't she who did the stabbing, although she'd wanted to, for a minute, anyway. What did Harry do to make someone else so mad? Was she in danger? She didn't have that eerie feeling one gets when they are. Surely the stabber would have come back for Rochelle by now, if that's what they intended.

Moosh bumped into Rochelle's leg and she hoisted him to her hip. "OK, Detective, I'll watch the recordings and let you know."

"Thanks, I'd appreciate that."

Rochelle hung up the phone and opened the door, walking into her back yard with Moosh in her arms. It was still drizzling. The garden beds were soaked from the torrential rains of the previous days, mulch was muddy and eroding, flowers' fragile stems were bent and leaning, pummeled by the bullying water droplets. Branches and leaves fallen from trees littered the once pristine grass. Her yard was in disarray, just like her life.

Rochelle placed Moosh on the ground to do his business. She made her way toward the fence at the back of the yard, afraid to peer into the makeshift nest, afraid of what she may or may not find. Thankfully, the baby bird slept quietly in his safe space while Mama watched from the rooftop, not too far away. "That's a good mama, you keep a watchful eye over the one you love."

Rochelle double-checked all gates were locked—she didn't want any more surprise visits from nosy, misinformed reporters. She headed back toward the house, "C'mon Moosh!" Moosh wobbled after Rochelle and the two went back inside, where the pup immediately curled up to take a nap on the sofa, gently collapsing his flexible cone as his sleepy head touched down.

Rochelle poured herself a glass of wine, took her glass, the bottle, and her laptop into the living room, and nestled in on one end of the plush the sofa. Moosh softly whimpered at the other end, kicking his tiny legs, one white and curly, the other pink, shaved for the IV. Rochelle watched his half-opened eyes roll in his head, as he faintly barked and twitched. She hoped he was chasing a squirrel in his dreams and not running from the scary memory of surgery.

She opened her email to see one from Detective Blankenship in her inbox. His message contained a link and a password that would send her to a page littered with even more links of video clips form Harry's surveillance camera. She took a sip of wine as she clicked on the first link. Not much to look at. The camera pointed down to the stoop outside the door to Harry's home office on the other side of their estate. Atop the stoop sat a coco door mat monogrammed with an elaborate *H*. The same style mat, in different sizes, graced all entrances of their home. This specific entrance was designated for Harry's work deliveries, which is why he was the only one who monitored the footage.

As Rochelle perused the list, all the videos were the same. Every few days, a delivery person would drop off a package or packages and at some point Harry would emerge—at least the top of his head and shoulders would, as he stepped out to grab the deliveries and bring them inside. From its bird's eye view, the camera would watch

Harry step out, squat for a package, and carry it inside. It became routine: delivery, Harry, squat, carry. Link after link Rochelle watched the same thing: delivery, Harry, squat, carry. Until she didn't.

In one of the clips, the camera was flipped, now pointing upward, showing nothing but Texas blue sky and the occasional wisp of cloud. Hours later, it was flipped back again, watching the stoop, and the monogrammed mat. A few other times it was swiveled upward. What was Harry doing? Once in a while he'd look up at the camera. Those were the times Rochelle would look away. She didn't want to see his eyes, however grainy from the low definition, looking at her. She clicked further.

What was that? A quick flash of flesh—at least some fingers, anyway, getting in the way of the lens before tilting it toward the sky. Was that Harry? There was not enough hand in view, not even a full finger. Maybe there were more clues to come? Rochelle clicked to the next video, nothing, and the next, nothing. Then, there it was again! Giving her a little more flesh, more fingers in view. Was the culprit getting lazy, brave or brazen? She paused the video when the doorbell rang.

MOOSH POPPED HIS HEAD UP, and groggily barked at the sound of the visitor, startling himself from inside his personal echo chamber. He hopped off the couch, forgetting about the oversized cone, and rolled heels over head. Rochelle picked him up.

"Be careful, baby," she examined his undisturbed stitches, "you are in no condition to be a guard dog." Rochelle tiptoed to her front door with the lights out, wondering who would be ringing at 9:00 PM. It was Maeve, who squealed at the sight of the pup as soon as Rochelle opened the door.

"Oh my gosh, look at this little turnip," Maeve scratched Moosh's forehead as she stepped inside. "He looks so cute in there."

"I know, adorable, isn't he?" Rochelle closed the door, peeking over Maeve's shoulder, thankful no vultures were lurking. The only thing left was her trampled front lawn.

"Cute as a button, honeybee, how's he doin'?"

"He's a little out of it, but haven't we all been?"

"Amen to that!"

Maeve followed Rochelle into the living room and sat on the sofa, placing her handbag on the floor. Rochelle placed Moosh back on his comfy spot and assembled some pillows on the floor below him just in case he decided to hop off the couch again. She retrieved another glass, and poured some wine for Maeve.

"Thanks, honeybee."

Rochelle clinked Maeve's glass with hers. "This is a late visit... Is everything OK?"

"Everything's fine," Maeve sighed and sipped. "I just wanted to check in on you," she scanned Rochelle, her gaze pausing at Rochelle's abdomen, "see how you're doin'."

Rochelle reached over to scratch Moosh, "I'm fine now, relieved actually."

"Roey?" Maeve's concerned blue eyes reminded Rochelle of tumbled sea glass.

"Yes, Maeve?"

"I hate to be annoyin' as a June bug, but, don't you think it's a bad idea to be drinkin' wine in your condition?"

"Maeve..."

"I mean, I thought about the other night and I feel darn awful about givin' you that pill. I just thought you bein' calm would be better for the baby than if you were all skeetered out."

Rochelle pursed her lips, and thought for a beat, "Maeve, there's something I need to tell you."

"You're mad at me? I realize, now, it was too strong for you."

The worry etched on Maeve's face made Rochelle chuckle. Rochelle grabbed Maeve's hands. "No, I could never be mad at you. Look at you, worrying about me every day, taking care of me."

"Well, you *are* my best friend."

"Yes, and that's why I need to tell you...I'm not pregnant."

"Oh no!" Maeve pulled her hands away, covering her mouth, "Are you OK? What happened?"

"I was never pregnant, Maeve." Rochelle felt slightly ashamed.

"What?"

"It was a white lie—a big lie, to get back at Harry."

"Well, what in the world..."

"I don't expect you to understand...considering. I just wanted you to know."

"Well, what in the world would Harry do, God rest his soul, that would make you want to lie about somethin' like that. I know how much you wanted to have a baby. I know how hard you tried."

"I don't know if I can talk about it right now, without falling to pieces, Maeve." Rochelle felt the heaviness of Harry's presence on her shoulders. "Let's just say, sometimes we think we know someone —*really* know someone. We can sleep in the same bed with them every night, and wake with them every morning. We can share our brightest hopes and dreams and also our deepest fears and vulnerabilities with them. We know their sounds and smells and can probably identify them blindfolded. And then, one day, they do something that surprises us, something completely out of character—teaching us we never really knew them at all."

Maeve took a sip of her wine and placed it on the coffee table. Her lower lip began to quiver and she burst into tears, "Oh Roey, I don't know what to do."

"I'm sorry, Maeve, I didn't mean to upset you." Rochelle rubbed Maeve's back.

"It's not you. It's Barrington. I think he's havin' an affair." Maeve rang her hands.

"An affair? You're always together. How can that be?"

"You just said it yourself, we can think we know someone and then we don't."

"I guess I did." Rochelle didn't want this to be true for her friend. "What gives you the idea he's having an affair?"

"I don't know. He's been actin' so strange lately, secretive, distracted—irritable."

"Could be the stresses of his job. I can't imagine running a billion-dollar company."

"It's not just that, look at how he's fightin' with Mirabelle all the time."

"Yes, but that's also on Mirabelle, you *know* she's so competitive, she likes a healthy debate. Small talk bores her. I actually think they get a kick out of arguing with each other."

"I guess so, honeybee. But what about him closin' his computer when I'm around, and havin' secretive phone conversations?" Maeve fiddled with the three small diamonds hanging from her delicate platinum necklace.

"Hmmm...that's a little worrisome."

Maeve reached down into her purse and pulled out the small white paper, "And what about this?" She pushed it toward Rochelle. "Read it!"

Rochelle hesitated to take the paper. "Oh, I don't know Maeve, the last time I read a paper that wasn't intended for me, things didn't end well."

"What are you talkin' about?" Maeve unfolded the paper and showed it to Rochelle. "Look! A phone number, and when I dialed it, a woman answered."

"Well, what did she say?"

"Not a darn thing. I got so flustered, I hung up."

"Let me see that?" Rochelle took the paper from Maeve and read it. The handwriting gave her a chill, the number seemed very familiar. Rochelle took her phone from the coffee table and started typing in the numbers written on the paper, as Maeve panicked in her peripheral.

"What are you doin'? Are you callin' her? What are you gonna say?"

Rochelle entered the number without pressing *dial*. "Nothing, look." Rochelle showed her screen to Maeve. The number was programmed into Rochelle's phone.

"I don't understand."

"This is Harry's attorney. This is Harry's handwriting."

"Oh my God, Ro, is Barrington havin' an affair with Harry's attorney?" Maeve clutched her chest and Rochelle laughed. "What's so funny?"

Moosh popped up and wobbled over, wanting to join in on the fun, bopping Rochelle with his cone. She picked him up and held him close. "Maeve," Moosh licked the air attempting to reach Rochelle's face, "Harry's attorney would rather have an affair with *you*, not Barrington. She's a lesbian. Harry probably shared the number with Barrington as a business referral."

"Oh."

Rochelle watched Maeve return to fiddling with her three-diamond necklace and remembered the story Maeve told her of the lovely gift. It was the first piece of jewelry Barrington ever purchased for Maeve, signifying his love for her, the three diamonds stood for *I love you*. Rochelle knew Maeve hardly ever took it off. "Did you even ask him, Maeve? About the number?"

Maeve's translucent skin turned from pearl to pink. "No." Her sea glass eyes lightened with relief. Rochelle felt relieved as well. There was no room within their little circle of friends for any more tragedy. At least that's what she hoped.

26

GROWTH

D ragonflies danced, flitting about while flirting with each other, hovering just above Rochelle's once lush, green lawn. She watched as they made their way throughout the previously pristine yard, left soaked and battered by the storm. It was of no mind to the graceful insects who kissed the surface of the water in the lily pond just before zipping back off again. Mesmerized by the dragonflies, Rochelle followed their movements as Moosh romped in the distance, gaining a new perspective through his imposed conical vision.

The previous days' rain flooded the beds with the newly planted red-leafed begonias, yet the resilient plants still stood firm, doing their duty, hiding the pink paper shreds of Harry's heartless lie. Rochelle wanted to forget, wanted to bury the memory in the dirt forever —hoping the earthworms would eat through the shreds and turn them to waste. But now, with this torrent of rain, she feared the torn paper would grow roots, strong pink roots reaching far and wide, gaining enough strength to push an eager pink sapling up through the fertile earth, growing quickly into a tall, pink, flowering tree. Taunting her with hearty blooms of Harry's lies. Rochelle willed herself to stand strong, to have no fear, for she knew a paper tree was fleeting, unable to stand up to the brutal gusts of a determined soul.

A knock on her back gate startled Rochelle, giving her flashbacks of the nosy reporter from *The Inquisitor.*

"Go away!" she shouted as Moosh yipped at the visitor.

"Mrs. Hawthorne, it's Detective Blankenship."

"Oh," Rochelle walked toward the gate, "sorry, Detective." Rochelle opened the gate for the detective as Moosh tried to sniff him, bumping into his shin with the edge of the cone. "Come on in."

"Didn't mean to startle you. I tried knocking on the front door. Did you get my email? Have a chance to look over the video clips?"

"Yes, I started going through them," Rochelle began to gather the fallen branches littering the lawn, the detective followed her with Moosh trailing close behind. "I've not made my way through all of them yet, there are so many."

"Did anything strike you as out of the ordinary?" He pointed to the wood. "Can I help you with that?"

"No, I'm fine." Rochelle was used to doing yardwork on her own. Harry never really enjoyed it, he would rather hire someone than spend his days off getting dirty. "I haven't noticed anything odd. Is that why you're here?"

The detective squatted down to give Moosh a scratch. "No, there's something else. I wanted to let you know your husband's body is ready for release. For you to have it back, for burial or a service." The detective stood.

Rochelle set the branches on top of the wood pile next to the outdoor fireplace. *I don't want it back.* "Oh, OK." She brushed the dirt from her hands. Rochelle hadn't even thought about what to do with Harry's body. Never mind have a service for him. *Celebrate him?* She didn't feel like celebrating his life of lies. She'd been so preoccupied. Her friends hadn't asked her about a service, maybe they'd skated around the issue to protect her. Maybe they thought it was too soon. Harry didn't have any family to remind her either, she was all he had. *Why wouldn't he want to have a child of his own to carry on his name?*

"Mrs. Hawthorne?" the detective touched her arm, snapping Rochelle out of her daydream.

"Oh, yes, um, thanks, Detective."

"Well, I'd better get going. Call me if you think of anything."

"I will."

27

AFFAIRS OF THE HEART

R ochelle sat at her dining room table, clicking through the uneventful surveillance videos, this time going back to the beginning and focusing on Harry. What had been going through his head all those years? His shoulders, they appeared broad and straight, but were they gradually bowing, ever so slightly, burdened by the weight of his lies? Was Rochelle able to detect a slight difference in his posture as she studied him, stepping out to retrieve his packages? She had a view from above, a guardian angel's perspective, unable to warn him, to tell him he was making bad choices, to protect him from his impending doom.

She paused the video and stared, stared at the top of Harry's head and shoulders, wondering about the angle of the camera. She rose from her chair and made her way out of the dining room toward Harry's office on the other side of the house. She passed through the living room, where large, leaded glass windows rose from floor to high ceiling, giving an exquisite view of her once beautifully flowering yard, where blooming crepe myrtles and Japanese red maples added color to the lush green lawn—beds that once exploded with blossoms were now healing from the storm.

Christopher's exquisite eye for design brought the nature she saw through her glorious windows into her living room, by helping her choose her supple sage green sofas, their calm color echoing the outdoors. She passed her master bedroom, also with large, leaded glass windows looking out to the yard. These had a view of the pond, and when she cranked the windows open at night, she could hear the chatter of frogs. Those same croakers remained invisible during the day, burying themselves deep into the flowered beds. Down the hall-way, past the indoor sauna, was the home gym, also windowed, fitted with a treadmill, stepper, various weights, and the Peloton bike Harry rode every day. Rochelle once wanted to build that room as a glass atrium, letting in all the day's light along with the beauty of her spec-tacular yard, but the hammering Texas hail put an end to that idea.

Not far from the exercise room was the door to Harry's home office. Rochelle opened the door and stepped inside, onto the intri-cately patterned Persian rug, inhaling the familiar scent of leather, bourbon, and cigars. She ran her hand along the handsome custom desk that sat quietly in front of floor to ceiling bookshelves buzzing with titles. This is where Harry would take his last-minute conference calls —the ones that would often make them late for dinner reservations. She ran her hand over the handcrafted rosewood, ebony, and mahogany desktop, able to feel the differences in the graining, as she thought about all the times she waited patiently for Harry, conferencing at his desk, knowing it would be selfish for her to get mad they were going to be late for their anniversary dinner. After all, if it wasn't for Harry working so hard, they wouldn't be able to enjoy such dinners. At least that's what he would always tell her.

The soaring bookshelves spanned every wall of the office, save for the one with the stone fireplace. In front of the fireplace sat a toffee leather sofa, she could see the indentations in the cushions, the place they sat, on chilly winter evenings with their feet up on the coffee table, in front of the warm fire, sipping brandy. Intimate evenings, where Rochelle would share what was on her mind, and Harry would keep his secrets from her.

The door leading out of Harry's office opened into a small court-yard, akin to the larger courtyard on the other side of their house.

Rochelle opened the door and stepped outside onto the monogrammed mat, where an abandoned package lay forgotten on the stoop. This part of the house backed up to a quiet, secluded road—a road whose existence was known only by informed visitors and private couriers. Large brick walls covered with green ivy surrounded and secluded the small courtyard. The walls were connected in the middle by an iron gate. Once a visitor typed in a code, given by Harry, they could enter the courtyard through the large gate and approach the delivery stoop, where Rochelle stood, looking down at the monogrammed mat, watched by the camera.

She picked up the lone package and turned to look up at the camera, which was just out of arm's reach, but able to be adjusted upward with a long-arm stretch on tiptoes. Rochelle wasn't sure why Harry would adjust the camera upward, especially if he was the only one reviewing the videos. Unless Harry didn't know Rochelle wasn't reviewing the footage...unless he was trying to hide something from her.

WHAT WAS THAT?

R ochelle clicked throughout the night, obsessively watching each and every mundane video clip. Boredom lulled her, tempting her to sleep. Ready to obey, her lids felt heavy, halfway closed, until she saw it—the flash. She rubbed her weary eyes to get a clearer look. There it was! A glint of metal that didn't belong to Harry. A wedding band perhaps? *Was Harry having an affair with a married woman? Could it have been one of her friends?* That would have been a good reason to adjust a camera out of view. Rochelle's phone rang, the number on the display told her she was going to need to make decisions about Harry's body.

PLEASE LEAVE A MESSAGE

Christopher dialed Mirabelle's number for the fifth time as he paced an indentation into the teak floor of his penthouse. "C'mon, c'mon, pick up, pick up!"

"This is Mirabelle, I can't come to the phone right..."

"Ugh!" Christopher hung up, plopped down on his sofa, and placed his head in his hands, clenching thick waves in his fists. His unlinked French cuffs flopped as he rocked back and forth trying to soothe his racing thoughts. "I can't remember, I can't remember," he chanted out loud to an audience of none.

Behind him, on his onyx kitchen countertop, stood the empty bottle of hundred-year-old scotch from Rochelle's birthday party. Next to that lay more empty liquor bottles. Scattered over his countertop, in his sink, and on his kitchen table, were others, their liquid as absent as the memories in his head.

DID YOU RING?

"**D**o you need to answer that?" Rochelle asked Mirabelle as Mirabelle stood on the doorstep, switching her phone to silent.

"No, it's just Christopher," she rolled her eyes. "He's called a hundred times already, probably fretting about what to wear to the service. That boy needs to relax. I'll call him back when I get in the car."

"Oh, OK, come on in." Rochelle led Mirabelle, followed by Moosh, into the dusty dining room, "Would you like a cup of tea?"

"Sure…" Mirabelle scanned the dining room as the sound of shovels scooping shattered marble emanated from the kitchen. "What's going on in here?"

The dining room, formerly adorned with exquisite antiques gathered by Harry and Rochelle from their travels around the world, now looked like some kind of battlefield. Atop the French 1920s buffet, an electric hot plate warmed a tea kettle. Next to it sat a separate automatic coffee pot and all the accoutrements of a local Starbucks—paper cups, cream and sugar, and little wooden stirrers stood at the ready. The green onyx Spelter mantel clock and two gilded Rococo candelabras, that once graced the buffet's top, now sat on the floor in a far corner of the room.

"Oh..." Rochelle pulled a tea bag from a drawer and placed it into a paper cup, poured hot water from the kettle into the cup, and returned the kettle to the hot plate. "I've been spending lot of time in here," she handed the cup to Mirabelle, who closed her gaping jaw. Rochelle turned and poured more coffee into her favorite mug, "The kitchen is still under construction." She sat at her end of the dining table, strewn with various papers and things, and started to click the keys on her laptop. "Sit, Mir."

Rochelle watched Mirabelle slide out the same chair she sat in the last time, her forgotten silk scarf still hanging from the back. Rochelle watched Mirabelle's hands as she pulled the scarf from the chair, shaking off the dust and tying it to the straps of her purse. "Sooo...you doing OK, Ro?"

"I'm fine." Rochelle took a sip from OH SHIT as Moosh curled up at her slippered feet.

"What are you working on over there?"

"Oh, just looking at videos from the security camera to Harry's office, trying to see if anything rings a bell."

"Great! Anything to help you find the person that did this to Harry."

"Yeah." *Anything to help find his mistress.*

"Any luck?" Mirabelle sipped her tea.

"No, not yet," Rochelle focused on Mirabelle's hands as her friend raised the paper cup to her mouth. The jade wedding band on Mirabelle's finger was far from the glint of metal on the hand of the visitor in the video. Plus, Mirabelle was much too short to reach the camera. Rochelle changed the subject, picking up the small plate of pastries in front of her. "Scone?"

"No, thanks, I've got to run to a Pilates class. But I'll take one to go."

"I'm glad you are going to be in town for the service, Mirabelle."

"Yes, me too, is there anything I can do for you?"

"No, thanks, I've got it covered. We'll come back here for dinner afterward."

Mirabelle looked around the disheveled room once again as the scraping from the kitchen continued. The drag of metal gave Mirabelle chills. "Are you sure you don't want one of us to host?"

Rochelle didn't look up from her computer. *Do I want one of you to host? NOW you ask? Where were all of you when it was my birthday? When it was time to celebrate me? I'll tell you where you were. Nowhere! Now you have the nerve to offer to host something for Harry? He's dead! Besides that, the lying bastard doesn't deserve it! Do you even know what he did to me? And besides, what did he ever do for you? I'M the one that slaved over recipes making sure that all of your gluten and nut allergies were addressed, while still serving food that didn't taste like cardboard. I'm the one who painstakingly assembled the floral arrangements making the environment suitable for your discerning tastes. I'm the one that burned my fingers bleaching your lipstick stains out of my linen napkins so you'd have something fresh to soil all over again. And now... YOU have the goddamned nerve to ask if YOU CAN HOST?* "No thanks, I've got it handled."

"OK, well, let me know," Mirabelle looked at her phone and rose from the table, "I've got to get to class."

"I will, thanks." Rochelle rose, and Moosh popped up, bonking his head on his cone.

Mirabelle giggled, "By the way, what happened to Moosh?"

"He had surgery, had a blockage removed."

"What kind of blockage?"

"He ate a ring, of all things."

"A what?"

Rochelle shuffled under the papers next to her computer to retrieve the ring. She slid it over to Mirabelle. "Here take a look."

Mirabelle looked down at the ring, a simple band with two stones, one sapphire and one ruby, handsome brothers sitting side by side.

31

WTF

C hristopher capsized the freshly folded pile of clothes, once neatly stacked on his sofa, as he dug for his phone lodged deep in the cushions. It was Mirabelle. He fumbled to answer. "Hello?"

"What the fuck, Chris?"

"Mir, I'm sorry for calling so many times but..."

"NO, what in the HOLY FUCK was your RING doing in the STOMACH of that dog?"

Christopher stood silent, brow crunched, "What are you talking about?"

"Your fucking ring!" Mirabelle screamed, flipping the bird to the driver of the other car who was staring at her as she idled at the stoplight.

"My ring?"

Mirabelle drew in a long, murderous breath as the light turned green. Slowly stepping on the gas, speaking deliberately, "Where...is...the ring...you had on...the night...of Rochelle's...birthday party?"

" I don't know."

She drew in another strangulated breath, and hissed, "I doooo."

"You do?"

"They RETRIEVED it from the STOMACH of her fucking DOG!"

"Whose dog?"

"Rochelle's!"

Christopher slapped his hand over his mouth, "Oh my God!" He started to cry, "Moosh is dead?"

"No, the dog isn't dead, you dolt! The little fucker is running around, in a cone, like an idiot."

"Oh, thank God!"

"Look, I don't have time for stupidity, I'm on my way to Pilates and then I have to pick the girls up from chess camp, so let's get to the big picture fast."

"OK...stop being mean."

"I'm not mean, Christopher, I'm a realist. If your parents didn't coddle you, you'd be way ahead by now."

"OK Mir, what's the big picture? And by the way, that ring means a lot to me."

"Why, who gave it to you?"

"It doesn't matter."

It really didn't matter, Mirabelle just wanted to know. "Okayyy...how did it end up at Rochelle's?"

"I don't remember."

"What do you mean you don't remember?"

"I don't remember," he paced his penthouse, "I remember having it on the night of her party. But after...after that weekend, I realized it was missing and thought it must have slipped off my finger when I was rearranging the flowers I brought. But it wasn't anywhere near there. So I tried other places. I've been panicked looking for it ever since."

"Is that why you were on her kitchen floor looking for your *contact lens*?"

"Yes...how'd you know that?

"Rochelle told me. Why didn't you just tell her the truth?"

"Because, Mirabelle, I didn't want to give her anything else to worry about after...after Harry." Christopher's throat seized as he pushed though, "It's such a tragedy. I don't know how any of us are going to recover from this. Oh God!" Christopher looked at the empty bottles on his counter, "Wait...how do you know? About the ring?"

"She showed it to me."

"Did you tell her it was mine?"

"No! The woman is losing it! She's living out of her dining room, in her pajamas, with her dog, serving tea from paper cups while her kitchen floor is being scraped into a wheelbarrow! I was afraid she'd seek revenge on you for almost murdering the dog."

"Oh, phew!" A moment of silence, "Wait...paper cups?"

CLICK.

32

THE SERVICE

Rochelle sat in the front pew of the small chapel looking every bit the grieving widow. She *was* grieving, for her dead child and all the other children Harry denied her. She sat, draped in a graceful black wrap dress and heels, her hair twisted into a fiery knot, antique diamond comb tucked inside. Moosh sat next to her in a little black suit jacket and bow tie.

The cloyingly sweet smell of flowers hung in the air as Rochelle inhaled deeply, welcoming in the syrupy fragrance, when something dawned on her. She thought about how often people associated the overwhelming scent of flowers with funeral homes. No matter where they were, if there was an abundance of flowers, they'd saying something like, *Ugh, it smells like a funeral home in here.* She believed it troubled them, maybe because it reminded them of death—the death of a human. But sitting there now, smelling the heavy bouquet, the combined varieties of beautiful exotic flowers, Rochelle realized something. It was the death of the flowers she smelled. Humans never smelled that lovely. It was the gorgeous and innocent flowers, that were sacrificed—decapitated, forced to sit alongside a dead, reeking human. It's the smell of innocence. The flowers' dying fragrance is their final gift to us.

Rochelle had time for these thoughts, sitting quietly in the pew. She stared at the mahogany and sterling silver urn housing Harry's ashes, as it sat atop a stone pedestal, surrounded by the beautiful, murdered flowers. It made her angry. Everything made her angry, lately, especially the burnt remnants of Harry, in his urn. The urn itself was a family heirloom—handed down from the nineteenth century, Victorian, one of a pair, valued at fifteen thousand dollars. It was handcrafted from mahogany, boxwood, and tulipwood, boasting beautifully turned acorn finials, adorned with a sterling silver shield embedded in front and engraved with an elaborate *H*. Rochelle knew what she wanted when the funeral director called.

"Hello, Mrs. Hawthorne? I'm Theodore Bundy, from Our Eternal Sorrows Funeral Home."

Wow, Ted Bundy...fitting. "Hello, Mr. Bundy."

"I'm so sorry for your loss Mrs. Hawthorne."

If only you knew what I've lost. "Thank you."

"I know there are a lot of decisions to be made during this process, but I'm here to help you, I'll hold your hand along the way."

"OK."

"You have several options for burial..."

Burn him. "Cremation!" She blurted out.

"Oh, uh, OK..."

"Harry always wanted to be cremated and sprinkled somewhere he loved." She lied, having no idea what he wanted, for he never talked about anything beyond the superficial.

"OK, well...then let's decide on a vessel."

"A vessel?"

"Yes, the urn that will house your husband's ashes. I've got a catalog you can browse through."

"Oh, I don't need that. I have one already, a vessel, a family heirloom, that meant a lot to him. We can use that."

"OK, that sounds perfect, sentimental."

Rochelle knew it was perfect, for the pair of urns were intended for cutlery. One for forks and spoons, and the other for knives. She thought the urn fitted for knives would be perfect.

"And the service?"

Rochelle didn't want to talk about the service, she didn't want to talk about anything else, so she tuned out the chatty funeral director until there was nothing left for him to say. Until she found herself sitting in the front pew of the chapel, with Moosh, resenting Harry in his urn.

Soon, she was surrounded by her closest friends. Maeve, Barrington, Mirabelle, and Christopher, along with a smattering of nameless, faceless people attended the private ceremony, as Rochelle sat in the exact spot she didn't want to be.

Later on, down the line, someone would plan another service for Harry, for all his business associates—something extravagant and over-emotional. Where people she wouldn't recognize would take her by the hands and pretend to be devastated, telling indulgent stories about a husband, she now knew, she didn't really know at all. A husband who didn't give her a choice, who deprived her of the child she would never get to love.

"Please, Harry, just think about it."

"Rochelle, stop being so selfish...we're not adopting. If you weren't so broken...broken...broken..."

Rochelle wanted Harry's service to be over, and soon it was. After tuning out the eulogy, it was time to bring it home. She lifted Moosh, holding him tight as she rose from the pew, making a little curtsy at the end of the bench, bowing to the plain wooden cross hanging on the front wall. She wondered if she was doing the right thing—curtsying to the Jesus-less cross before approaching the lectern. This was a chapel, not a church, was there a difference? She carried Moosh and walked right by the burnt pieces of Harry, deposited in the priceless family urn. She walked right by and mourned—mourned the flowers, dying by the crumbs of her dead husband.

CLEARING HER THROAT, Rochelle stood at the lectern, holding Moosh, adjusting the microphone with her free hand, as the squeal of feedback echoed throughout the silent chapel.

She looked out into the pews, to see her friends—Harry's friends, quietly adding coughs and sniffles to the soundtrack, as devastation distorted their faces. She watched them as they watched her, patiently waiting to hear the loving prose she'd prepared for her lying, murdered husband.

"It's hard for me to stand here and talk to you about Harry. It's hard for me to put into words exactly what I feel about him at this very moment. One can't expect a grieving wife to stand in front of a grieving crowd and keep it together, to say the right things about a husband who is no longer here. So all I will say is...it feels as if we were married forever and yet not long enough. There was so much more...*so much more* I needed to learn about my husband. But time did not afford me that opportunity. I hope to, someday, learn from you...his friends...what Harry meant to you. The little things, *every little detail*, that made Harry who he was. Wherever he is, I hope that his eternity is filled with *everything* he gave to me. Especially the last few days of Harry's life, the last honest moments we spent together. That's all I can think to say."

With all eyes on her, Rochelle stepped down from the small altar, placing Moosh on the floor, holding his leash as they walked toward Harry's urn. Rochelle lovingly reached out, in the direction of the urn, and picked up the lovely floral arrangement sitting beside it. Leaving Harry's urn where it was, Moosh's lead in hand, Rochelle carried the floral arrangement with her as she walked down the aisle and out of the chapel.

33

DINNER WITH HARRY

They all sat in silence around the dining room table —Rochelle's friends. The men, in their bespoke suits and shirts, tailored to perfection, cut from Egyptian cotton and Italian wool, and the women in their couture dresses of sewn spun silk and handwoven brocade.

Barrington's conservative charcoal-gray suit was simply styled, with a paisley silk tie and pocket square to match, both in varying shades of gray, complementing his white hair. Christopher's plaid Gucci suit, also shades of gray, was embroidered with little silver bees, his vest, contrasting in pattern only, was scattered with flowers. The rims of his glasses were mother-of-pearl and matched the large floral pin poked into his tie.

Mirabelle wore a solid black dress spun from Chinese silk, as the hint of a dragon, embroidered in black thread, whispered throughout. Maeve's brocade dress was an intricately handwoven charcoal and silver fabric, flowing like liquid over her form, flattering her voluptuous figure. Haute couture, in respectful, muted colors carefully chosen by their owners, made Rochelle's friends appear as if they were living in a black and white film. The only thing thumbing its nose to the respectable palette was the grotesque sea of diamonds and pearls accessorizing their looks. Accessories they thought they needed to be worth something.

They all sat in awe around the dining room table, in astonishment of the table-scape—or lack thereof. It was something new, something Rochelle had never done before. Nothing. The fancy friends sat quietly, looking out of place, around the bland and dusty candle-less table, where nothing sparkled and nothing shone. Where plain paper plates replaced hand-painted heirloom china, paper cups replaced stemmed cut crystal and plastic knives and forks replaced monogrammed sterling flatware. A roll of paper towels lay at one end of the table, while mismatched casseroles, filled with unrecognizable food, lay at the other. Food, sent by those who weren't invited to Harry's service.

The only decor were floral arrangements, those sent in sorrow, and those Rochelle removed from the chapel. She carefully placed them around the room, giving them the respect they deserved. They were, after all, sacrificed, to honor her lying, dead husband. She placed the biggest, most beautiful one on the Chippendale buffet, next to the warming plate and coffee pot.

To make room for the arrangement, she removed Harry's urn from the buffet and walked it over to the far corner of the dining room, placing it on the floor next to the discarded candelabras and clock, as her friends watched in disbelief.

"Who's hungry?" she asked, returning to her end of the uninspired table and pouring some wine into OH SHIT.

Barrington was the first to awkwardly break the silence. "I am." He grabbed the casserole closest to him and tried to scoop a pile of food with a little plastic spoon; the head of the spoon snapped under the weight of the food and he grabbed another.

"I need a fucking drink," Mirabelle whispered under her breath to Christopher, picking up a bottle of red wine and filling herself a paper cup.

"Me, too!" Maeve said, holding out her paper cup for Mirabelle to fill.

"Don't forget me," Christopher said, nodding at his empty cup and forking a slice of beige meat onto a plate.

Dinner resumed as usual, with a little bit of eating, a lot of drinking, and volatile arguments between friends.

"ARE YOU KIDDING ME?" Mirabelle yelled over the phone at Grandma, who had the nerve to ask if the twins could go swimming. "Put them on the phone! Yes, Mama, both of them!"

Christopher silently motioned to Mirabelle, asking if he could have her dinner roll. She fluttered her eyelids, practically shooing the roll off her paper plate with a dismissive hand gesture as she waited for the girls to come to the phone. "Absolutely not! No... Did either of you finish your booklets for math camp?... I didn't think so... Lily don't ask again... I'm not mean, I'm teaching you responsibility, which you are obviously too dumb to get... Ivy...Ivy, stop crying... I didn't call you dumb, I was calling your sister dumb... Yes, I know you're twins... Yes... I know you're identical...just because she's being stupid, doesn't mean you are... NO...that doesn't mean you get to go swimming instead...put Grandma on the phone..." Mirabelle rose from the dining room table and took her call into the other room.

"Pshaw...'bout time," Barrington shook his head, attempting to spread a pat of hard butter on a soft roll, snapping his plastic knife. "Fuck."

"Lordy, baby, lemme help you with that," Maeve reached over and took the roll out of his hands. "It was a beautiful service, Roey."

"I guess it was...nice flowers, anyway." Rochelle sipped from OH SHIT, hardly remembering the service.

"I was wondering why you didn't have any of Harry's employees there." Maeve handed the nicely buttered roll back to Barrington.

"I'm sure the office will go ahead and plan something. I just wasn't up to all those people...honestly, I don't even know most of them."

"All those techies?" Barrington popped the whole roll into his mouth, "Probably just a bunch of flaming liberals if you ask me."

"Excuse me?" Christopher sat dumbfounded.

Maeve pinched her husband and whispered, "Don't. Start."

"Ow! Excuse what? Is *flaming liberal* a gay slur too? Am I going to be allowed *any* words?"

"You, sir, are a Neanderthal." Christopher shook his head, spreading some orange cheese from a nut-covered ball onto a cracker.

"Besides," Rochelle continued, while stabbing a thick piece of meat with a plastic fork and laying it on her paper plate, "I can't help but think, they all think I'm the one who stabbed Harry." She picked up her plastic knife as her friends glanced at each other.

Mirabelle reentered, phone in hand, and placed it on the table. "Sorry, guys."

"Why don't you put that thing away?" Barrington nodded at her phone.

"Why should I?" Mirabelle sat, transferring wine from her soggy paper cup into a fresh one.

"Because it's so disruptive, and it's rude, and no one wants to hear you yelling at your kids."

"Oh *really*?" Mirabelle addressed the table, "Is anyone here upset that I yelled at my girls?"

"Well..." Christopher started to speak, and Mirabelle kicked him under the table.

"And if I wasn't the one who stabbed Harry," Rochelle attempted to slice through the thick slice of meat with her plastic knife, "then I can't help thinking, it must have been one of you."

Christopher choked on his wine. Barrington belly laughed at the thought, and a troubled Maeve addressed Rochelle, "Are you serious, honeybee? Is that what you think? That one of us would hurt Harry?"

"You've got to be joking," added Mirabelle.

"She *is* joking," Barrington boomed, then addressed Rochelle. "Right?" All eyes were on Rochelle, who was still sawing, barely making an impression in the tough cut of meat.

"Well...Detective Blankenship told me the knife used to stab Harry was one of my Wüsthofs from the kitchen. So, the weapon came from inside the house. If I wasn't the stabber—and I wasn't—it had to be one of you." She pointed with her plastic knife, then resumed sawing.

"Because there was no break-in, and Harry wouldn't have let a stranger into the kitchen."

"You're serious?" Barrington asked.

"Yes! She's serious!" Christopher snapped. "Jesus, are you that thick?"

"Fuck you, why are you such a little bitch?"

"Don't attack him like that!" Mirabelle defended Christopher.

"I'm just telling the truth, he's always a little bitch."

"Barrington!" Maeve scolded.

Rochelle discarded the dull plastic knife and tried another.

"The truth? When have you ever told the fucking truth?" Mirabelle shot back. Christopher nudged Mirabelle under the table. "What?" She glared at him.

"Shhh!" His widened eyes pleaded for her to stop.

"No, I will not shush!"

"Mir..." Christopher hissed through clenched teeth.

"Christopher! Stop being such a pussy!"

"Whoop! There it is!" Barrington tried to joke, but Mirabelle was on him fast.

"Fuck you, Barrington! All these years, you've sat across the table with your holier than thou attitude. Making *me* feel bad for pushing my girls to be their best...gloating about your boys making it into Harvard without much effort."

"Mir..." Christopher placed his hand on Mirabelle's arm.

She jerked it away without looking at him, "No!" She kept her focus on Barrington. "Gloating about your boys...throwing it up in my face...how *easy* it was for them..."

Barrington coolly sat back in his chair, sucking air through his teeth, leaning back on the chair's legs. "It *was* easy for them, they're naturals."

"Where are you goin' with this, Mirabelle?" Maeve asked.

"You husband...the big shot billionaire and his antics...don't act like you don't know."

"Don't know what?"

"Ugh...she doesn't know, Mir." Christopher smacked his own forehead, "I'm such an idiot for telling you!"

"Don't know what?" Maeve repeated.

"Well, maybe she should!" Mirabelle tilted her head, challenging Barrington.

Barrington settled the chair back down, his eyes jutting back and forth between Mirabelle and Christopher, who was chugging his wine. "You don't know anything," he taunted the two.

Mirabelle stood, pushing her chair out from behind her with the back of her legs. Her small frame leaned over the table as she rested forward on her open palms, pushing all her energy toward Barrington. "I...know...everything...I know you paid to get your boys in to Harvard."

"Ha! No, I didn't. Don't confuse that with a mere donation to the school."

"Everyone donates, Mirabelle." Maeve stood in solidarity with her husband.

Mirabelle's eyes narrowed, darkening like a deadly storm, "Right...but a donation to a FAKE college-prep foundation, where the ringleader connects with and BRIBES COACHES. Say...oh...I don't know...ROWING COACHES...to recruit students onto their team roster, when they DON'T EVEN ROW FOR THE SCHOOL? THAT is something completely different!"

It took a minute for it to sink in—the accusation. Maeve turned to her husband, "Did you do that, baby? Did you bribe the rowin' coach to get the boys into school?"

"Nope, I didn't bribe anyone."

"*You* didn't bribe anyone but you paid someone else to do it. What was his name again, Chris?"

"I don't know what you're talking about." Christopher refilled his wine.

Mirabelle glared at Christopher, who seemed unwilling to help her cause.

Barrington continued to push Mirabelle's buttons. "Besides, the boys also have perfect SAT scores, so they would have gotten in either way."

Maeve cringed at her husband's comment; she knew Barrington's boys were not gifted academically.

"Look!" Mirabelle pointed to Maeve, "Look at your wife's face! Even she knows that's a lie! You probably had someone take their SATs for them."

Barrington glanced down at his Hermès tie, softly whistling while fiddling with it. "No one will ever prove it!"

"OH MY GOD! FUUUCK!" Mirabelle screamed, stomping her foot, causing Moosh to bark from the other room. "I hate you!" She sat down hard.

Barrington leaned forward on the dining room table, "Why all the hate, Mirabelle Huang-Chung—heir to a Chinese real estate dynasty, married to an heir of a Chinese real estate dynasty. You guys are loaded. I can hook you up...relax. Then you'll finally be able to ease up on those girls and let them live their lives. Let them go swimming, for God's sake!"

"What? Pay? That's disgusting...I would never do that! Never cheat! Never teach my girls to cheat!"

"Plus...you'd go to jail for that anyway," Christopher added, transferring his wine to a fresh paper cup.

"Bullshit...no one will go to jail," Barrington boasted. "It's a donation to a charity, as far as anyone knows! Nothing illegal happening here."

"But, that's not true, now, is it Barrington?" Christopher added. "People *will* go to jail in due time. Especially because it's been found the charity is fake. I know for a fact indictments are being drafted as we speak. Indictments for *all* involved."

"*Indictments?*" Barrington scoffed.

"Yes...indictments...right now...to nab cheaters like you!"

"On what grounds?"

"Money laundering and racketeering and I'm sure there's more. You know it and I know it."

"And how do you know all this? Is this the gossip running among the interior design sector? In between pillows and poufs?"

"HARRY TOLD ME…" Christopher blurted, causing Mirabelle to give him an elbow, "…before he…Harry told me."

Rochelle set down her dull knife and excused herself from the table, "I need to check on Moosh."

Christopher eyed Rochelle sheepishly, as she walked out of the room, calling to her, "I'm sorry, Rochelle."

"Is this true, Barrington?" Maeve stood over her husband. "Is *this* why you had the number for Harry's attorney in your pocket?"

"Uh…well…no…I mean…how do you know about that?"

"I have friends, Barrington Avery Spencer!

34

GROWING ROOTS

Arguing voices faded as Rochelle left the dining room. Her chest hurt, wrenched with anxiety. She hated her current situation. Hated the way she was behaving. Hated the way her friends were behaving. She couldn't believe she'd suggested one of her friends would hurt Harry, it just came out that way. She didn't plan it, nor did she expect to say it, she didn't even know where it came from, but she couldn't take it back. Her emotions were a roller coaster, she didn't recognize herself anymore.

She opened the door to the mudroom where Moosh excitedly waited on the other side. She didn't have the heart to put him in his crate, not with that contraption on his head. "C'mon baby, want to go potty?" She picked him up and carried him out the back door, settling him onto the grass. A tiny lizard popped its head up and scurried away, and Moosh followed after. Still dressed from the service, Rochelle kicked off her uncomfortable heels and nestled her feet into the damp grass. The cool earth under her feet felt so good. She closed her eyes and took in a long, deep breath, inhaling all the fragrance of her garden —flowers and trees and earth, it was impossible to be anxious in this space. She focused on the bottoms of her feet and imagined them sprouting roots, imagined driving them down deep into the soil, planting herself, becoming one with the fertile loam that lay beneath the surface. In turn, she felt the earth giving back to her, sharing its grounding energy, giving her peace of mind and balance.

She wished all her friends would come out and do the same. Surely that would ease their tensions, quiet their frustrations. Why were they arguing all the time? Why was Mirabelle so worried about her girls getting in to Harvard? They weren't even in high school yet. What if Ivy wanted to be an artist or Lily a poet? Would it matter they didn't earn their degree from Harvard or Yale or Stanford? Would it make them less of a poet, less of an artist? Would the girls, in turn, be *less than*? What about Barrington? His kids were at Harvard already and no matter how they got there, it seemed to be Barrington's accomplishment, not theirs. If the boys weren't at Harvard, would Barrington be *less than*? And Christopher, he had a hard time because he was a gay man living in an ignorant world, a world telling him that because he was gay he was *less than*. Why would any of them believe they were less than perfect just the way they were? Maeve was the strongest of them all, she would never let anyone tell her she was anything less than what she was. She was a smart, confident woman, with a beautiful soul, and Rochelle admired that about her.

Rochelle opened her eyes and scanned the yard for Moosh. She giggled when she saw he had a butterfly visiting inside his cone, his little eyes were crossed, ogling the creature so close to his nose. He nervously sneezed to shoo it away, but the butterfly just sat there, confident in who it was, patiently raising and lowering its wings, until it was ready to fly away, on its own terms.

Rochelle took in another long, steady breath and blew it out just the same. Surely her friends would be finished arguing by now. "C'mon Moosh." The little dog followed her back into the pantry. "I love you, baby." She gave him a treat and closed the door.

~

THE SQUABBLING HADN'T STOPPED, it had actually gotten worse.

Rochelle let out a heavy sigh as she walked back into the dining room, her damp, bare feet still tingling from the good earth.

"Wait a minute…" Christopher was half drunk now and slurring accusations at Barrington, "You were the one who was s'pposed to meet with Harry the day he was murdered."

"Christopher, that's enough!" Rochelle scolded her friend, who was in no condition to listen.

"No, Rochelle, lizzen…he…" he softly pointed at Barrington, "he…was the one who was meeting with Harry that day."

"Don't be ridiculous!" Barrington chided. "You're drunk!"

"No…no…no…" Christopher shook his head with woozy eyes, "You have motive. You must have been mad as hell that he knew all about…*hic!*…all about this fake college stuff."

"Sweet baby Jesus!" said Maeve.

"Christopher, settle down." Mirabelle placed her hand on Christopher's arm.

"Nope…" Christopher slowly pulled his arm away from Mirabelle, pointing a gentle finger at her. "You're pretty…" he squinted at her, "but lizzen to me…you're a bisch." Mirabelle rolled her eyes. "You…" He pointed back at Barrington. "You're the one…"

Barrington looked at Rochelle, "Rochelle, don't listen to this drunken fool."

Christopher didn't stop, "Harry *told* me you were going to meet with him. He *knew* you were going to be indicted soon, and you must have known, too, that's why you wanted to shut him up! You wanted to make him go away, so he wouldn't tell anyone."

"Bullshit, you're making no sense! I had no knowledge of any indictments."

"Lizzen to yourself, you sound so guilty…" Christopher's head moved like an old tortoise as he turned to face Rochelle. "Ask him, Rochelle, ask him if he stabbed Harry."

All eyes were on Barrington as he explained, "Look, Rochelle, there *were* rumors that a whistle blower may have leaked information about the charity…about it not being kosher. But that's all I knew. I was just looking for legal advice, just in case."

"AHA!" Christopher stood from his chair and stumbled right back into it. Mirabelle placed a heavy hand on his arm.

"That doesn't mean anything, Christopher," Rochelle walked to the buffet, switching on the automatic coffee pot. "You need to sober up."

Barrington turned to Maeve and took her hands in his, "Yes, pumpkin, that's why I had the number of Harry's attorney in my pocket. Harry was trying to help me retain counsel if this were to turn into a shit storm. I was supposed to meet with Harry the day he...later that day...but he never showed."

"Why didn't you tell me?" Maeve's sea glass eyes grew dark.

"Because, I didn't want to worry your pretty head. This doesn't involve you."

"Yes, it does involve me. This is *our* life. I'm your wife."

"Who knew nothing about this...you are not involved. I'll see to that."

"And what about the boys? Did they know?" Barrington opened his mouth to answer but Maeve touched her fingers to her husband's lips, "Never mind. Don't answer that. Whether they knew or not, they are now involved. Why did you have to cheat them in? What good is it gonna do them now...once everythin' comes out?"

"I don't know." Barrington poured himself a shot of whiskey and downed it as he watched Christopher's glazed eyes stare through him. "What about *you*?" Barrington glared back.

"What about me?" Christopher adjusted his mother of pearl frames.

"Where were *you* that weekend?"

"I was working on a big project."

"Where?"

"Uh, in Dallas."

"That's vague, especially for a man who elaborates on everything. What project was it?"

"It was...uh..." Christopher rubbed his forehead and squinted, his buzzed mind searched for the words...searched for the memory.

"We'll, what project was it?" Barrington insisted.

"It was...uh..."

"It was *what*?"

"I don't remember!"

Mirabelle watched her friend's hand massage his crinkled brow —his ringless hand. A jolt of adrenaline shot through her. "Oh my God," Mirabelle slapped her own mouth, trying to stop the words she accidentally let escape.

"What?" Christopher looked at her.

"Nothing." She shook her head quickly, not wanting to finish her thought.

"You look like you've seen a ghost, Mirabelle." Rochelle took her seat at the table. She addressed Christopher, "The coffee will only be a few more minutes." He did not hear her, he was distracted, focusing on Mirabelle.

"What, Mir?" Christopher asked again.

Mirabelle shook her head quickly, again, wishing Christopher would just hush.

"C'mon Mir..." Christopher playfully poked her, "pretty bisch...what were you going to say?"

Rochelle saw trepidation in Mirabelle's sparkling black diamond eyes. Mirabelle looked at Christopher, her very best friend, giving him a sad smile, the sparkle in her eyes waning just a bit, as she whispered, "Your ring."

Christopher stopped, sobered by the thought. He looked down at his ringless hands and then, nervously, at Rochelle. She didn't get it at first, but then...a gut punch. She quickly stood from the table and approached the buffet, knowing something was dreadfully wrong, but she wasn't sure what. Rochelle's heart pounded in her chest as she unsteadily poured black coffee into a paper cup and placed the pot back on to its warmer. It was Christopher's ring? Christopher's ring that the doctor had to fish from Moosh's intestines? If it *was* Christopher's ring, was Christopher there the day of the stabbing? Was *he* the stabber? Maybe Harry wasn't having an affair with another woman, maybe Harry had something on Christopher. Rochelle's head spun with confusion. She felt nauseous, taking in deep breaths to calm herself, holding on to the banquet to steady her stance, closing her eyes, trying not to hyperventilate as she opened the top drawer to the buffet, her bare feet longing for the comfort of her yard.

Mirabelle nervously shredded the paper napkin at her plate. "Christopher, when did you lose your ring?"

"I lost my ring...I think...during Rochelle's birthday dinner, but...but, I can't remember..."

Rochelle's hand shook as she placed the black coffee in front of Christopher; next to it, she settled the ring. Christopher silently stared into the black void of coffee as he slowly placed his hand over the ring. Closing his eyes, a tear escaped.

35

A RING AND A PROMISE

Rochelle watched Christopher gaze at the ring, looking as if his spirit had died. Christopher barely eked out a whisper when he asked her, "Where did you find this?"

"In Moosh..." she answered, "in Moosh's bowel. He *somehow* ingested it."

"What...what did I miss?" Barrington was confused. "Your dog ate *what? How?*"

"Shut up!" Maeve whispered to her husband.

"I have no idea how," Rochelle answered, suddenly irritated as she looked at Christopher. "Do *you* know?"

"No, I...I don't. I...thought I lost it the night of your party."

"I don't even remember you wearing this at my party." Rochelle glanced at Maeve who gave her a sympathetic smile. "I guess I was too buzzed to notice."

"Yes, Christopher had it on the night of your party. I remember admiring it...wait a minute," Mirabelle poured Christopher's leftover wine into her own cup, "you were too buzzed? I thought you weren't drinking because you were pregnant."

All eyes were on Rochelle, Maeve was the only one who wasn't confused. "I slipped." Rochelle stared at the ring in Christopher's hand. "Put it on," she said, hoping to quickly change the subject.

"Put what on?" Christopher asked.

"Put the ring on your finger!" Rochelle demanded.

Rochelle watched as Christopher fumbled, with shaking hand, to slide the band onto the ring finger of his left hand. Rochelle felt numb as she watched Christopher choke back sobs.

"What are you blubbering about?" Barrington asked. "It's just a stupid ring."

"It's not a stupid ring!" Christopher cried, head in his hands, trying to catch his breath in between uncontrollable sobs.

Mirabelle rubbed Christopher's back. Maeve stood and walked around the table in an attempt to soothe Christopher as well, "Oh, sweet pea."

Rochelle wasn't having any of it as she stood at her end of the table. "Turn your hand over!" she demanded of Christopher.

He looked up. "What?" he asked, surprised at her tone.

"Turn your hand over!"

Christopher turned over his hand, and Rochelle walked toward him, grabbing his left hand to get a better look at his palm and fingers. Her stomach wrenched. There it was. The glint of a band from the surveillance video was now in front of her, wearing the blob of flesh it belonged to. "*You're* the one?"

"He's the one, what? What *am* I missing here?" Barrington asked.

Christopher lowered his head. "I'm sorry, Rochelle, Harry was going to tell you."

"Oh my God, Christopher!" Mirabelle stood.

"Yes, Christopher!" Rochelle added, "How in the world was Harry going to tell me anything, after you stabbed him multiple times?"

"What?" Christopher stood from the table and stumbled backward, bumping into the buffet behind him, barely saving the large floral arrangement from falling. He hyperventilated, "No... I didn't stab Harry..."

"Then how did your ring end up in *my* house, *in my dog*!"

"You don't...understand..." Christopher tried to speak between gulps of air, "Harry…Harry…I would never hurt Harry…he…he…was going to tell you…"

"Tell me what?"

"That we were in love!" Christopher sobbed.

Barrington rose from his chair, "AH! I'm going to be sick. What in the hell is he talking about?" He looked for anyone to answer.

"In LOVE?" Mirabelle threw her hands up, "The man was having a baby with his wife, for fuck sake!"

Rochelle could not control her thoughts, her blood boiled, reddening her face. "STOP SAYING THAT!" She lifted the arrangement from the buffet and crashed it to the ground to make her point. "I'M NOT PREGNANT!" She barely missed Christopher, who quickly ducked away, running to the far corner of the room.

"Oh my lord, honeybee, settle down!"

"Then why would you tell us you were pregnant," Mirabelle was confused, "tell Harry you were pregnant?"

Christopher stood in the corner, looking down at Harry's urn as Rochelle answered, "Because he was a liar! He was a COWARD and a LIAR!"

Christopher picked Harry's urn up from the floor and hugged it, closing his eyes. Rocking with it in his arms.

"Put that down!" Rochelle said, approaching Christopher.

"No!" He opened his eyes and stepped away from her.

"Give him to me!" She unsuccessfully reached for the urn.

Christopher pulled it away, "Why should I? You don't care about him! You barely said two meaningful words at his service, didn't invite any of the people who love him, and basically tossed him on the ground!"

"Give her the damned urn, Chris!" Barrington chided.

Christopher backed away, grabbing the urn tightly, as Barrington joined to help Rochelle.

"Give him to me!" Rochelle insisted, grabbing the finial top. "He's my husband!"

"I will NOT, I am the one who loves him!" Christopher held on tightly to the middle.

"Don't be an asshole, Chris!" Barrington grabbed the base of the urn.

They all tugged, each pulling at whatever parts they could keep in their grasps. "Christopher...let...go!" Rochelle pulled up on the urn, knocking Christopher's glasses off his face and onto the ground, as Barrington pulled down. Christopher leaned back with all his might, trying to fight both of them off. All that pulling disengaged the top and bottom from the middle of the antique—the middle that Christopher held steadfast in his grip, the inertia hurtling him backward as he tripped over his own feet, falling to the ground, as Harry's ashes scattered everywhere. A cloud of Harry drifted in the sunbeams of the waning light streaming in through the dining room windows. Enlightenment.

Rochelle watched Christopher, lying on his back, covered in the soot of her dead husband, hugging the broken worthless urn, sobbing, as his tears carved rivers into the ashes his face. She wanted to feel that pain, that pain for her lying, cheating, dead husband. But all she felt was pity—pity and stupidity. She felt nothing more as her husband's lover felt everything, his head somewhere else, tangled in some memory.

HARRY HELD the black velvet box toward Christopher and opened the lid, revealing the most beautiful ring—the most beautiful ring Christopher had ever seen. They sat at a candlelit table in a darkened corner of the New York restaurant. A weekend rendezvous, where the aroma of Italian food comforted the soul.

"I want you to have this," Harry said. "I had it made for you." Christopher couldn't believe what he was hearing. "It's a symbol of us. One sapphire and one ruby, my birthstone and yours, together in an endless band. Signifying our infinite love for one another." Harry held up his hand, "I have one too."

"Oh my God," Christopher held his hands to his mouth, "it's gorgeous."

"Well, give me your hand."

Christopher held out a shaking hand, and Harry slid the ring onto his finger. Christopher stared at the beautiful, slim band and the gorgeous stones—emerald cut, one blue, one red. Christopher pulled Harry close. "I love you so much." He pressed his lips onto Harry's beautiful mouth—forbidden kisses were the most intoxicating.

Harry cradled Christopher's chin as he looked into Christopher's eyes, "I know it's been hard, hard for us both, hiding like this. But I promise you I'm going to make things right. Do you hear me? I'm going to talk to Rochelle when I get back and tell her I want a divorce. I need a divorce. I'm done hiding."

Christopher hugged Harry tightly, closing his eyes to retain every beautiful image of the moment. "That makes me so happy...*you* make me so happy."

Christopher's heart ached with love for Harry. He'd waited years for Harry to finally work up enough courage to tell Rochelle he was gay. He was also sick of hiding—and all the lying, it was exhausting. It was also torture not being able to touch Harry when they were out together in public, relegated to stealing glances when no one was paying attention. Brushing hands against each other when no one was looking. He knew it was going to be hard for Harry. Harry loved Rochelle, and so did Christopher, he knew it was going to be hard on her because he knew what it was like to love Harry. He couldn't imagine what he would do if he didn't have that love.

As Christopher looked down at the ring on his finger, he felt his spirit soar. He was finally going to be able to spend his life openly, with Harry.

36

NOTHING

Rochelle watched Christopher as he lay on the dusty floor of her dining room, coated by the eruption of Harry's ashes. She watched him, curled into a fetal position, rocking to sooth himself as he hugged what was left of the urn, crying uncontrollably over her lying, dead husband.

Rochelle envied Christopher. Not because he'd had an affair with Harry, but because he felt so much. She envied his emotion. Rochelle was numb. She felt nothing for Harry. Harry ripped her heart out, making her void of emotion, when he insidiously took away her ability to have their child.

37

HARRY

H*arry...*
What did she just say? I tried to rise from my seat, but I couldn't control the rush of adrenaline; it was crippling my weakened legs as I dabbed the sweat from my brow. *God, it's fucking hot in here.* I couldn't breathe, not after that verbal punch hit me right in the gut. *I'm pregnant*...that's what she said. Pregnant? How could that be?

She walked toward me—the birthday girl, looking every bit the Hollywood vixen, slinking my way, in her sexy silk dress. She made me sick, in a good way. Perfect tits and ass, the body of a goddess—a goddess with a fucking vengeance. Her hazel eyes stung like bees as she pierced my skin with every tiny dagger she hurled my way. There she was, leaning in, her full kissable lips this close, hot vodka-laden breath in my ear, driving me crazy. Yes, I'm gay—I'm not dead, I appreciate my sexy wife. *"Surpriiise,"* she whispered. Another verbal left hook, I was knocked back into my seat.

I felt nothing, numb like Novocain, while the rest were so excited, congratulating Rochelle, congratulating me. Barrington nearly broke my hand with that fucking overbearing grip. Everyone was so happy for us, everyone except me, that is, and Christopher. I could feel his stare, burning a hole in me, from the other end of the table. I didn't dare look...I didn't want to see my lover's beautiful, disappointed eyes. It'd kill me to see the damage those two words had done to him. I refused to look at Christopher. That is, until Barrington ordered Chris to fill everyone's glass with hundred-year-old scotch—a pretentious drink from a pretentious asshole. Christopher came to fill my glass, and I couldn't down it fast enough. "Can I have another?" He ignored me. I didn't blame him. I'd ignore me, too.

Get me the fuck out of here. I had an urge to run, but there was nowhere to go. I was stuck, imprisoned by my own doing. I'm such an idiot. I should have told Rochelle years ago, should have just confessed. I love men, another man, actually. And yet, I still love my wife. And now she's pregnant? How? I'm going to sue that doctor, muddy his name for his incompetence, and take him for all he's worth. Did they tell me a vasectomy might not be one hundred percent effective? I'm going to have to consult the paperwork buried deep in the lining of my briefcase.

Unless...unless, it isn't mine? She cheated? No, Rochelle would never cheat. She's bigger than that. I'm the cheater. There I sat, in a room, on my wife's birthday—my now-pregnant wife, with my sad lover and my asshole friends. I was stuck. Maybe I was the asshole. I wondered what was for dessert, maybe I could gorge myself to death with petit fours. I felt like I was going to pass out. I loosened my tie, the tie my now-pregnant wife gave me, or did Christopher give it to me? I can't remember. The gifts are starting to blend into each other.

I finally found the courage to look at Christopher, he was filling Mirabelle's glass. Her manservant—I was beginning to think Christopher relished playing the role. That's what I liked to tell myself. I was jealous, really. Jealous of Mirabelle and all the time she got to spend with Christopher. I wanted that time, but I couldn't have it. It wasn't fair. The ringing of Mirabelle's phone snapped me out of my self-pity.

She was pissed. I wondered why the hell couldn't her kids watch television. She needed to loosen the rope on those two—never in a million years. There she was, yelling at her mother. Mirabelle was always yelling at her mother, she was always yelling at everyone. She liked to spar. Personally, I loved that about Mirabelle. She wasn't fake.

Barrington was taunting Mirabelle about finishing their conversation. Barrington was fake as shit. But he was about to go down, and he didn't know it. He was caught up in an impending scandal—a college scandal, where prominent assholes were actually paying colleges and coaches and SAT institutions to lie and cheat and steal. Anything to get their rich little brats into school. Little brats that weren't going to study. They were going to drink Everclear until they puked, they were going to ditch class to shoot heroin and take selfies. They were going to steal the spot from a deserving kid, a poor kid, who had all the brains but no chance in hell, because they had no money, and that wasn't fair. I was glad those cheating assholes were going to pay. It was about time.

I gave Barrington the number of my attorney; she was an animal, but Barrington was fucked either way—money laundering, racketeering, mail fraud? He'd end up spending a few years behind bars, depending on how he played it.

Yes, Mirabelle, flip Barrington the bird! I love it! Mirabelle, the one who told the whole world to fuck off. I was glad she was leaving, glad because that meant Christopher was leaving, too. I needed some time to process this news. I'd deal with Christopher later.

Barrington slapped me on the back, almost making me spit out my teeth. Fuck! Calling me *my good man*, was I good? I think I broke a rib. He wanted to smoke some Cubans and have a little bourbon while, as he said, the ladies could "catch up and talk babies!"

Ugh...I almost forgot. Wait, what about the scotch?

"Ah," Barrington said, striking a match on the underside of his ostrich skin boots, and speaking through the puffs as he lit his cigar, "Christopher...*puff*...that little bitch...*puff*...he took the scotch...*puff*...*puff*."

I wanted to punch that fucking cigar right into his homophobic face. But that was going to have to wait.

∾

I SNUCK into the bedroom and knocked my shin on the hard corner of the bed. Fuck. Every fucking time. I disturbed Moosh, who growled at me long and low. "Shhh, Moosh, it's just me. Don't wake Mommy." I watched as he stood and adjusted himself, curling up into a ball in the opposite direction, nudging his back even closer to Rochelle. How was that even possible? Those two were inseparable. I stood still for a minute, holding my breath, terrified I was going to wake her. *Please, no.* I was drunk and exhausted and not in any condition to have a meaningful conversation.

Barrington. God, that guy's a piece of work. I spent the whole night outside with him, cringing, forcing myself to listen to one narcissistic story after another. Not even the warmth of the fireplace could make it better. My only saving grace was the bourbon—Redemption, what a fucking fitting name. Warm and smooth as it went down, it numbed my body. My mind was elsewhere, worried about Christopher. I should have been worried about Rochelle. Instead, I avoided her. I needed time to think. I knew the night was over when Maeve came out to tell us Rochelle had put herself to bed, said she wasn't feeling well.

"Must be that little Baby Hawthorne growin' inside," Maeve sang.

I felt sick to my stomach. I wanted to retch. It was either that, or the cigars and the booze. It could have been Barrington's stories. I couldn't wait to lock the door behind Maeve and that asshole. I dug in my pocket and pulled out my cell. No calls. I dialed Chris and he fucking denied my call—the first one, the second one, all fifteen. Fuck it. I eventually gave up. I'd call him in the morning, which was just a few hours away.

I lifted the sheet, felt like a naughty teenager sneaking back in after curfew as I slowly slid into the bed, trying not to wake Rochelle. She was out like a light, breathing heavily, her back to me. I knew I wouldn't sleep much. My mind was full...restless...racing. But Rochelle, she was sound asleep, every once in a while I felt her foot twitch. I imagined she was dreaming of the baby. I would be dreaming of Christopher.

38

STALLS

Christopher stumbled into the stall of the dank restroom, slamming the door behind him, carrying the half-empty bottle of hundred-year-old scotch. A dying fluorescent tube flickered above, strobing the cockroach trapped in its case. It was one of the seedier gay bars in one of the worst parts of town, and somewhere Christopher wouldn't be recognized.

Drunk and claustrophobic, he held on to the metal walls of the stall, covered in torn posters of cabarets-gone-by and sharpie graffiti. He pressed his arm outward against the sticky metal to try to keep the room from spinning. The wait was torturous. He slid to the filthy floor. The putrid stench of urine and semen caused him to vomit into the even filthier bowl. When he was finished, he wiped his mouth on his plum jacket and sat against the door of the stall, hugging the bottle, too inebriated to stand. He removed the small wax packet from his pocket and unfolded the paper, revealing the powder. She said it was safe. But how honest could a woman named *Mad Dog* be? Christopher didn't care. He had nothing to lose—nothing but two days, because that's how long his bender would last. He blacked out as he tried to forget about his lover's pregnant wife.

39

SNEAKING OUT

I opened my eyes and zeroed in on a billowing strand of dust. Watching, as it hung on for dear life, clinging to the end of the blade on the motionless ceiling fan, like a mountain climber who'd lost his grip and was hanging on with only the calloused fingertips of one hand. Was that me? Clinging onto what was left of the facade of my life? It was fucking amazing, really—that filth, dust upon dust, amazing how, over time, it grew from a speck to a thread. If it wasn't tended to, it would eventually become a network of webbing. Just like my fucking lies. Starting with one...a lie to myself...and then to Rochelle, until there were more. Lie after lie, entangling me in my own fucking fabric of stupidity. I could have stayed there forever, watching it, reviewing my mistakes in my mind...but I didn't have that luxury. I needed to escape.

I held my breath, afraid to make a move, afraid to wake Rochelle as I slowly turned my head to look toward her side of the bed. She slept, still in the same position, her back to me, her red hair screaming at me. I envied her slumber. I slowly lifted the sheet, sliding out of bed without making a sound. Moosh quickly popped his head up, sleep in his eyes, still at the ready to guard his mistress. "Shhh..." I whispered, holding my fingers to my lips, as I tiptoed out of the room, closing the door behind me.

The sun wasn't up yet. My mind raced all night thinking about Christopher and wondering where he was, thinking about the baby, thinking about Rochelle. I knew it was all she ever really wanted. It was all she ever talked about throughout our marriage, every minute she could, until I told her to stop. I didn't want to hear it anymore, couldn't bear the pain in her voice, the longing, the fucking desperation. I felt bad, but I knew it was one dream that wasn't going to come true for her. I couldn't justify bringing a baby into our relationship when I knew it wasn't going to last. Because…I was going to tell Rochelle I was gay, that I was leaving…I was going to tell her. Until I fucking didn't.

I felt like such a coward. I should have told her that first year, that first year of marriage when I had too much to drink and fucked that guy in the bathroom stall. I was a drunken asshole, but it opened my eyes to something I had been hiding for years, something I was too ashamed to admit to myself. I was going to tell her. But I didn't. One year of marriage turned to one and a half and then Rochelle was pregnant…until she wasn't. I didn't mean to yell at her about the move into our new house, but, when I walked in, there was so much clutter. Looking back, it wasn't the crumpled papers and the opened boxes with items scattered everywhere, it was the clutter in my mind that made me angry. I was living a lie and there was no escape. But I did yell at her, and she did suffer a miscarriage. Whether it was my fault or not wasn't the point. The point was, Rochelle was gutted, and I couldn't leave her, not just yet, not when she was that devastated.

I did, however, take it as a sign and quietly made an appointment to have a vasectomy, finding a doctor who didn't require my wife's consent. It was my way of making sure I could control the situation. Making sure nothing would lock me in, knowing, at some point, I could leave. It made me a bit nervous, the finality of it all. But, in no time, it was over. That evening I hid it from Rochelle as best I could, pretending I pulled my groin muscle when she rolled over wanting to try again for another child. I played that card until I was fully healed. I would tell her my truth, as soon as *she* healed emotionally. But two years became three and then three became six. And then...I met Christopher.

He was actually Rochelle's friend first, Rochelle's and Maeve's and Mirabelle's. A talented interior designer, hanging out with his lady-friends. He became a regular in our little dinner club of six, with Christopher filling in for Mirabelle's husband, Chao, who was always away for long periods of time on business. It didn't matter to Chao that his wife spent a lot of time with Christopher, Christopher was gay...and so was I.

It all started when Rochelle hired Christopher as a designer to redo the interior of our house, to pick out couches and curtains and shit. I didn't care about any of that stuff. I knew Rochelle had great taste. Her vision, coupled with an interior designer? I knew things would turn out well, I'd just sign the checks. It was all going well until it came time to spruce up my office. Rochelle had a suggestion.

"Harry, why don't you and Christopher go shopping for a sofa for your office?" She said. "He and I talked about it and we think it would be nice for you to have one in front of the fireplace."

"Can't you do it, babe?" I asked her. "I don't really know what to pick. I'll go with whatever you choose."

"No, sweetie, *you* pick," she insisted, "this is your space. I've had say of the whole house, I want you to find something that speaks to you."

Fuck. That was the last thing I wanted to do, shop for a couch. But I agreed. Little did Rochelle know, the thing that would speak to me, the thing I would choose, would be Christopher.

"Look, Harry," he said. "I know you don't want to shop for furniture." He had me pegged.

I told him it's not that I didn't want to, I just had shitty taste.

"No worries, my friend," he assured me, "I know the most fabulous sofa for the spot. What do you say we just go out for a nice long lunch, so Rochelle thinks you're shopping. This way you won't be in the doghouse for shirking your duties. She'll think you picked the sofa yourself, and I'll have it delivered to your office." He chuckled, placing his glasses over the greenest eyes I'd ever seen.

I told him it sounded like the perfect plan and thanked him for helping a guy out.

We ate at a restaurant in the design district. It was odd and eclectic, kind of like Christopher. We took our time, grazing on a little bit of food and downing a lot of shaken cocktails. It was long enough for me to get to know Christopher on a deeper level, as a friend. He was quite a character. I liked him a lot. In a weird way, Christopher reminded me of Rochelle. He was kind and talented and funny.

I remember almost pissing my pants, "The Sausage King?" as I laughed hysterically.

"Yes," he told me, "that's the business my great-grandfather built, a hundred years ago, and it's still going strong!"

"Well, that's fitting isn't it?" I said, eating the olive from my martini glass.

"What do you mean?" he asked. He was confused.

"I mean…a gay man…inheriting a business called The Sausage King," I couldn't catch my breath. It was fucking hysterical.

Christopher feigned offense as he raised his hand to his chest, "Oh my God, Mr. Hawthorne, are you making a homophobic joke?"

Shit. I stopped laughing. I felt terrible for offending Christopher. "No…no…I'm so sorry. I didn't mean to—" I stuttered like a fool.

"I'm just fucking with you," he said. "It is fucking hysterical." We laughed all through lunch and all through the drive back.

"Yes," he told me, standing in my office, in the spot where the couch would eventually sit, "the sofa will be perfect here. It's smooth and supple nubuck leath—"

I grabbed Christopher. I couldn't help it. I planted a passionate kiss on his lips. He pulled away at first, but only for a split second. He pressed back into me, returning the deep kiss

In the blink of an eye—how can *two years go by in the blink of a fucking eye?* I ran my hand along the supple nubuck sofa, as I stood in my office, where Christopher and I made love for the first time...two fucking years ago. I forced myself to swallow the bile, bourbon and cigars from the night before, as my stomach wrenched, thinking about how *he* must have felt at Rochelle's pregnancy announcement. I needed to talk to Christopher, and then to Rochelle. I was done lying, I was going to make things right, if it was the last thing I did.

My office chair creaked, reclining ever so slightly under my weight as I clicked on the bankers lamp. I opened the top drawer of the desk, digging far into the back, finally excavating the small black velvet box. I lifted the lid, revealing the ring. It was a simple band, with two stones, emerald cut, one ruby and one sapphire, handsome brothers—a match to the one I'd designed for Christopher.

I removed my wedding band from my finger, knowing the promises it symbolized, the promises I made to Rochelle, the ones that died long ago—along with my honor. I fucking hated myself. I stared at my unadorned finger, at the band of lily white flesh that remained, untouched by the sun, staring back at me, scolding me for all I didn't do, for all the hurt I'd caused. *No more!* I ached for a new start. I slid the custom band, with its sparkling stones, over my finger and placed my wedding band into the velvet box, snapping it closed. I placed the box in the drawer, pushing the drawer forward until it clicked shut.

I reached across the desk and pulled my old briefcase toward me, settling it onto my lap. As I opened the top flap of the satchel, the faint hint of adhesive solvent tickled my nostrils. I removed the files and paperwork from inside, placing them on the desk, turning the case over, hovering it above the desk, allowing pens, pencils, and smaller items to fall out, littering the desktop. I opened the soft leather wider to get a better look inside the bag, reaching down into the satchel to lift the leather lining, to remove the thing I'd hidden so long ago. *No more secrets, no more lies...what's this?* The lining had been glued and sewn shut. Perplexed, I removed the letter opener from its stand on my desk and started to pry away the stuck lining, forcefully snapping threads with the pointed tip, freeing the stitching, until the edge curled up once again. I pinched the curled corner of the lining and pulled hard, lifting strands of adhesive as the lining gave way from the walls of the old satchel.

It was gone! The pink paper I'd so carefully folded and tucked inside all those years ago, was no longer there! In its place, a square indentation, worn into the leather over time, a shadow of its former self, the only proof the thing once existed. She knew!

40

SHEETS

T he sheets were not familiar to Christopher. Neither was the boudoir lamp draped with the sheer, floral, fringed shawl. However, the empty bottle of scotch on the end table was. Christopher groaned as he turned over in the bed, half blind in his right eye, a migraine vice tightening his skull, trying to focus. Slowly, a face came into view, at his level, head on the pillow next to him, and…two black spiders?

"Hey baby," the gruff voice whispered.

Christopher opened his dry mouth to speak, but no words came out.

"There, there, baby," the voice's rough hand rubbed Christopher's free shoulder, his other shoulder was buried, pushed into the musty mattress, "Mama will get you feelin' alright again, you had a rough night." The spiders were moving.

"Muh…my…my glasses?"

"OK, beautiful, " the voice's body leaned over Christopher to reach the end table, crushing him deeper into the mattress, giving him a taste of the acid in his stomach. "Here you go…" the voice placed Christopher's glasses onto his face.

A clearer view—no spiders, just thick false lashes gracing the face of a butch bar queen. Her black corset cut into her hairy, meaty frame as she reached over to the end table on her side of the bed. Christopher tried to push himself up and out of bed, but a wave of nausea and lethargy forced him back.

"There, there," the queen held out a tiny spoon piled with white powder, "this will help get you back on your feet in no time."

Christopher hesitated, this was not who he was, but then again, neither was Harry. Christopher sniffed.

41

CRUEL INTENTIONS

Moosh sniffed around at my feet as I made myself some coffee and scrambled eggs. Where the fuck did yesterday go? It was already Sunday morning and Rochelle was up before me, rising before I'd managed to drag myself out of bed. I didn't hear her get out of bed, I must've been dead to the world—the sleepless nights finally catching up with me. I inhaled the steam from my coffee, hoping it would give me a clearer perspective on the shitty situation I created.

Rochelle barely said two words to me before grabbing her keys and heading out the door. I didn't blame her, I'd be pissed at me too. It wasn't typical for her to be up this early on a Sunday, that was her day to sleep in. But then again, it wasn't a typical weekend, it was a goddamned nightmare and there was no waking up. How I fucking wished I would just wake up!

Rochelle hadn't said ten words to me since her pregnancy announcement at her birthday dinner, which made me feel like shit, and I wasn't making things any better. Maybe I shouldn't have avoided her calls yesterday afternoon, but honestly, I was scared shitless to face her, didn't want to see her devastation. I'd left her a note—wow, I really was an asshole. But, I needed to escape before she awoke, I wasn't sure of what to say to her. And now it was her turn to escape, made obvious by her early exit.

It was apparent she found the paperwork for my vasectomy in the lining of my briefcase. She must have hated me. I imagined her, stabbing the needle through the fabric, wishing it was my skin, slowly piercing it, drawing blood, as she sewed the lining back into place—I definitely received the tightly stitched message...loud and clear!

Wait a minute! It dawned on me, if Rochelle found the paperwork, then maybe she wasn't pregnant after all. Could she be fucking with my head? Trying to get back at me for being a shitty asshole of a husband? Wow! I was impressed. What a fucking badass move! I didn't blame her, she deserved to make me sweat.

I needed to find Christopher to let him know. I went out to look for him yesterday, but he was nowhere to be found. He wasn't at his apartment or answering his phone. I even called Mirabelle because it wasn't uncommon for him to crash at her house.

"Hello," Mirabelle answered in a huff.

"Hey Mirabelle, it's Harry."

"Hi Harry! Fun dinner last night, so sorry I had to leave early." Mirabelle's voice muffled, *"Girls! Get your rackets and get in the car!* Sorry...I'm running to drop the girls off at tennis camp."

"No worries, I was just wondering if Christopher was with you."

"Uh, no, I haven't seen him since last night. *Yes, Ivy, the blue racket.*"

"You haven't?"

"No, the driver dropped me off first. *Get in the car.* He did say something about not being tired after Rochelle's party, he probably hit a club."

"And you haven't spoken to him today?"

"*Seatbelts!* No, I haven't, but I don't usually have time to chit chat on Saturdays, the girls have a full schedule. *Lily! Stop hitting your sister!* Is everything OK?"

No, everything is not OK, it's a fucking shit show." Uh...yes, everything's fine. I, uh...just had a referral for him."

"He's probably sleeping off a hangover! He *was* enjoying Barrington's scotch on our drive back."

"Hmm, OK, thanks."

I poured myself another cup of coffee. *Come on Chris, it's been almost two days!* Maybe Christopher skipped town for the weekend, and I wouldn't fucking blame him. I'd give him another day, and then I'd start to worry. Besides, I still needed to have a conversation with Rochelle. Get to the bottom of everything. I hoped she'd be back soon. I picked up my phone from the counter and dialed my attorney.

"Sherri Kleinfeld."

"Hey, Sherri, it's Harry Hawthorne."

"Harry! How are you doing?"

I'm a fucking mess. "I'm good. You're all business on a Sunday morning."

"Harry, I'm all business all the time, which is why you probably keep me on retainer! What's up?"

"I just wanted to give you a heads up on a referral I'm sending your way."

"Ah, thanks for sharing the love!"

"Don't thank me yet. He's a friend of mine...a real asshole, but his wife is a good friend of Rochelle's. So I'd like you to help him out if you can."

"Sure, what's his story?"

"His name's Barrington Spencer, bought himself into a bit of trouble, cheating his kids into college. I think some indictments are coming...racketeering, mail fraud, money laundering...that sort of thing."

"Ah! Juicy! Is he well endowed? In the pocketbook?"

"Yep!"

"Well, then, any asshole of yours is an asshole of mine! Send him my way."

"Will do...don't hate me for it."

"Ha! Who could ever hate you Harry?"

I placed my phone on the counter and scraped the tepid eggs from the pan onto my plate, returning the pan to the stovetop as Moosh tap danced on the floor at my feet begging for a treat. I grabbed a spoonful of the eggs and crouched down to give him a nibble. Moosh ate the eggs from the spoon, then growled. "Hmmm, what 's wrong with you?"

That's when I saw him. Christopher was standing in my kitchen, drunken and disheveled, in the same clothes he was wearing the night of Rochelle's birthday dinner. He looked like shit.

42

CLEANING

C hristopher watched Harry's muddied ashes circle into the shower drain and disappear, along with his future. Harry was gone. Christopher felt lost. Mirabelle was soon to be on a flight to China, and his relationship with Rochelle had fallen apart. Poor Rochelle, he felt awful for the way things were, for their argument, for damaging Harry's urn. That wasn't the way he wanted Rochelle to find out about him and Harry—that wasn't the way at all. He'd begged Harry to tell her sooner, practically in the beginning of their affair, but Harry didn't have the guts. Maybe Harry was afraid to be honest with himself.

Christopher towel dried his hair and placed the towel back on the warming bar in his bathroom. He pulled on a pair of lounge pants with a matching top and slipped his feet into a pair of house shoes. Christopher lifted the ring from the silver bowl on the bathroom vanity and looked at the inside of the polished band, a tiny engraving, the name *Harry*. This was not Christopher's ring, this was Harry's ring, the identical mate to Christopher's, but he wasn't going to tell anyone, especially Rochelle. If she hadn't looked closely enough, then she didn't deserve to know. He slipped the ring onto his finger, the larger size easily clearing his knuckle, feeling content he had at least something, some part of Harry, as he switched off the light, and exited the bathroom.

In his kitchen, he began to survey the mess in his townhome, the mess he hadn't tended to in almost two weeks. *Ugh.* Depressive procrastination wasn't his friend. Empty liquor bottles littered his countertop, reminding him of *that* weekend, the weekend he ignored Harry. He was sick with guilt, knowing Harry was trying to contact him, while he was off getting blackout drunk, trying to forget about Harry's pregnant wife. *Harry's pregnant wife.* It was easier to stay mad at someone who didn't have a name, who wasn't your friend. Harry was gone, and Christopher never had a chance to say goodbye. He'd never forgive himself for that.

He tossed the empty liquor bottles into a large green garbage bag, filling the bag and tying it, placing it outside his front door. He wiped off the countertop with a warm soapy rag and swept and mopped his kitchen floor. Christopher moved into his living area where he spritzed and wiped the remnants of white powder from his glass coffee table. *Never again.* Christopher felt ashamed of what he now realized was immaturity and weakness. He should have conversed with Harry that weekend, instead of hiding. He should have answered Harry's incessant phone calls, or replied to a text. Maybe Harry would still be here. Instead, Christopher avoided...the details escaped him.

Christopher pulled the vacuum from the hall closet and started to pass it over his large Persian rug, thinking about the conversation he and Mirabelle had, while driving away from Rochelle's party.

"What the fuck is wrong with you?" Mirabelle frowned at Christopher as he drank the scotch from Barrington's bottle.

"Nothing, why?" He wiped liquid from his chin.

"Uhm...I don't know...you're drinking scotch from a bottle like a hobo. All you're missing is a brown paper bag!"

"Sorry," Christopher offered the bottle to Mirabelle, "do you want some?"

"Jesus, no!" Mirabelle tapped on her cell phone.

"You want to come out with me?"

"Come out where?"

"I don't know, a club...I'm too wound up to go home."

"I can't, I've got to get home and check on—"

"I know, you've got to *check on the girls*." Christopher mocked Mirabelle, rolling his eyes, as the car pulled up to Mirabelle's house. "You know, Grandma *is* capable."

The driver got out and opened the door for Mirabelle.

"Christopher," Mirabelle stepped one foot out of the car, looking at her friend. "I'm not sure what's swirling around in your mind, but I think you'd better quit while you're ahead. Go home." She kissed her friend on the cheek.

"OK, Mir, call you tomorrow."

"Not too early," she turned as she walked away, "the girls have a busy schedule!"

The driver shut the door and got back into the car; closing his own door, he turned to Christopher, "Home, Mr. Campbell?"

"No...take me downtown." Christopher took another swig of scotch, coughing at the burn as he tried to drown the words *I'm pregnant* out of his mind.

Pushing the vacuum, Christopher tried hard to remember where the driver dropped him off that night, and what he had done that entire weekend, other than ignore Harry. The only thing he remembered was waking up naked on his bathroom floor, two days later, surround in his own vomit.

Christopher passed the vacuum along the carpet, soothed by the monotonous back and forth of it all, until he hit a bump. He locked the vacuum handle, beaters still turning, and squatted down to pull up a corner of the rug, expecting to smooth a crumpled rug pad.

43

FORENSICS

A head peeked through the door of the detective's office, "Detective Blankenship?"

"Yep, come on in!" The detective stood from his desk, waving in the officer, who carried a clipboard and several manila envelopes.

"Hi, Detective, I'm Smith, from down in forensics."

"How can I help ya, Smith?"

"Uhm, I've got something for you, uh, that was uh, taken during one of the evals, the uh," the officer double checked a sheet on his clipboard, "the Hawthorne case? A stabbing?"

"Yes, I know it. What do you have for me, and what do you mean misplaced?"

The officer rolled his eyes, "We had an intern working with the M.E. The kid was a real doofus, who, uh, tried to lift a ring, exhumed from the throat of the victim."

"What?"

"I mean, the kid didn't actually take it from the vic's throat. The M.E. did, but the little thief swiped it afterward. He was stealing valuables, if any, from the cases he assisted...changed the paperwork and everything. We finally caught him, found all the shit in his locker, now we're trying to do catch up...yours truly being the delivery boy." The officer handed the envelope to the detective.

"Thanks...and you say this was in the vic's throat?"

The officer lifted a paper on his clipboard. "Yep. Laryngeal X-ray of posteroanterior and lateral view shows foreign object at vocal cord level. Should be on the envelope as well."

"Anything else?"

"No...and sorry about the delay, Detective."

"Not your fault, thanks."

Detective Blankenship sat at his desk and opened the envelope marked *evidence,* allowing the band to slide out onto the desktop. The detective picked up the ring, a slim band with a ruby and a sapphire. He turned it to look inside the band, needing a closer look with a magnifying glass, he read the tiny engraving—a name, Christopher. The detective picked up the phone and dialed Rochelle.

44

STASHED

With the stationary vacuum still whirring behind him, Christopher pulled back the corner of the Persian rug, confused he didn't find a crumpled rug pad. Instead, he found his plum jacket, his pants and shirt, from almost two weeks ago, stashed underneath. Each flattened piece of clothing was soiled, spattered with some type of brown sauce, and smelled of body odor and vomit. Christopher turned his head and gagged in disgust.

Vacuum still whirring, Christopher gathered the pieces of rancid clothing from the floor, the odors bringing him back to his forgotten weekend. As he lifted the jacket, something fell onto the floor—a clang of metal. He reached down to grab it, as different scenes started strobing, fading in and out of his mind. Entering a darkened club...music thumping...pounding shots...one after another...music thumping...handing a folded bill in a darkened hallway...a waxed paper packet in return...head thumping...puking in a dirty stall...snorting powder...head thumping...dancing in the darkened club...music thumping...sweaty bodies all around...music thumping...French-kissing strangers...bodies thumping...passing out in a cab...bodies thumping...waking up in a stranger's bed...heart thumping...snorting more powder...heart thumping...stabbing Harry...

45

WHAT JUST HAPPENED

"Jesus, you scared me!" I approached Christopher. Moosh was already at his feet, sniffing his shoes. He looked strung out as fuck as he stood before me in the kitchen, his clothes soiled and rotten as curdled milk. The putrid stench emanating from his body turned my stomach. "What the fuck, Chris? I've been trying to contact you for two days!"

"Don't come near me!" He pointed at me, hand shaking uncontrollably, darkness and tears in his bloodshot eyes.

It stopped me in my tracks, the way he looked at me, the way he was behaving. I tried to focus on his eyes, his pupils were as large as saucers, distorted behind the smudged lenses of his glasses, "What do you mean, don't come near you?" I held out my arms, "C'mon Chris." I tried to approach again.

"NO!" Christopher stomped his foot, scaring Moosh, who ran under the kitchen table and curled into a ball, tucking his head under his paws. "You stay away from me! I don't want you to touch me!"

"Please, let's talk." I couldn't fucking believe it. His hair was matted and greasy, it looked like he'd been sleeping on the streets.

"Talk about what, Harry? Your *pregnant* wife?" Christopher waved his arm in the air and stumbled as he looked around the room.

"She's not here, Chris. Please, let's talk. I'll stand right here, OK?" I tried not to move a muscle.

"*I'll stand right here, OK,*" he mocked me, "you, stand on the moon, you alien." He started to cackle maniacally, making no fucking sense at all. "Don't you talk about me...alien."

"Christopher, you're not making any sense. What have you taken?"

My heart broke watching the tears streak his soiled face as he held his fingertips to his bottom lip, nervously tapping, "Let's see, what have I taken? I have taken too much of your shit...*that's* what I have taken."

Good point. I closed my eyes and took in a deep breath, trying to stay calm, trying not to gag on his stench. "Where have you been, Christopher?"

"I don't know, but I know where I am going..."

"Where are you going, Chris?"

"I am going fucking *crazy*," his eyes widened with the words, "you have made me *fucking crazy!*" He started to punch his own head in frustration!

I quickly approached him, grabbing his wrists before he hurt himself. "Stop it! You'll hurt yourself!"

"Why?" Christopher's breath reeked of vomit and alcohol as he fought to free his wrists, but his weakened state was no match for me, physically. His words, on the other hand, were painful. "YOU have hurt me! What do you care, if I hurt myself?"

"I care...oh my God!" I struggled to keep my grip, turning my face to avoid his breath. I noticed a large hickey on Christopher's neck...a purple punch to my gut. "Where have you been, Christopher?"

"You said we were going to be together."

I actually had the fucking nerve to feel betrayed, that's how fucked in the head I was. "Where have you *been?*" I asked him, releasing his arms—hard. "For two days! And what have you done?" I honestly didn't want to know. I didn't think I could handle the truth.

"What have *I* done?" Christopher started to cry, then laughed psychotically, he was unhinged. "I have done *everybody!*" He presented his arms, spreading them, ringmaster fashion, accentuating his betrayal in grandiose fashion.

"Argh! Fine!" I was pissed, because hurting was weakness. At that moment, I hid my weakness behind my anger. "Is that the way you want it to be?" I removed my ring from my finger, the one that signified my love for Christopher, and held it up in the air. "THIS, was a promise to you! If you can't be mature enough to sober up and talk it out like men, then we have a real problem!"

Christopher's black eyes grew wide as he snickered at me, slowly clapping his hands, out toward me, mocking me. "Brava!" He performed for an audience of one. "SO dramatic! I'm not sobering up for you, I'm *never* sobering up for *you*!"

"Fine with me! Be a fucking asshole!" I slammed the ring into my plate, pushing it deep into the eggs, "It's over!"

I thought he'd call my bluff. Instead, Christopher lost it. He pulled off his own ring and barreled toward me, knocking the plate of eggs onto the floor, attempting to shove his own ring into my mouth, trying to silence me. "Don't say it! Don't say it!" He repeated, his eyes wild with uncontrolled fury. This was not Christopher, this was something else, something evil. I tried to fight back, but he found a strength I could not match. "Shhh..." He hissed, as he pushed the ring further into my throat with his filthy fingers. I gagged, smelling sewer and ass. Christopher's arms felt inhumanly strong as he pushed the ring further into my throat. I was choking. I couldn't catch my breath. Desperate, I grasped for anything to fight back, I found the knife on the countertop —anything to fight back.

Christopher's dark eyes cut to my fumbling hand and grabbed the knife first, plunging it into my side. Or at least I thought he did. I stepped back in shock, unable to feel the wound, unable to speak, having trouble breathing, still choking on the object lodged in my throat. Christopher, out of his mind, saw blood blossom through my white tee. "NO!" he screamed, stabbing at it to make the blood stop, forgetting he was still holding on to the knife.

Adrenaline rising, he struck again, and again, and again...

VACUUM STILL WHIRRING, Christopher screamed at the bloody knife in his hand, throwing it across the room, suddenly remembering what he had done, falling to his knees, "Noooo...noooo...noooo...noooo," remembering the look on Harry's face. "Noooo..." Christopher wailed, howling like a wounded animal, burying his head into the putrid clothing covered in dirt, vomit, and Harry's dried blood, screaming from the depths of his soul, collapsing onto the floor, next to the vibrating vacuum.

46

TIDYING THE NEST

Rochelle used a Q-tip to carefully dust the rest of Harry's ashes from the gilded crevices of the ornate Spelter clock, as Moosh, free of his collar, stretched out in the sunbeam on the floor under one of the large dining room windows. Rochelle placed the impeccably clean clock in between the two large candelabras on the buffet, blowing a strand of fiery hair out of her eye. It actually felt good—starting to put things back in order, back to where they belonged. If she couldn't control her circumstances, she could definitely control her surroundings.

It took two days to sweep and mop Harry's ashes from the dining room floor. As soon as she thought the house was clean enough, more dust would settle, thinly coating everything. It was typical Harry, always wanting the last word. She felt bad about her argument with Christopher, she wanted to be angry with him, but it seemed Harry was lying to both of them. In a way, they shared a kinship—she and Christopher, they both loved a liar, they were both left cleaning up the ashes.

Rochelle's phone rang, the caller ID told her it was Maeve, "Hi, Maeve."

"Oh honeybee…" Maeve sounded distraught.

"Maeve? Are you OK?"

"They took Barrington."

"Who took Barrington?"

"The authorities, they came to the house and charged him with all those things Christopher was talking about."

"Oh, Maeve, I'm so sorry."

"They put him in handcuffs and everything…it was awful."

"Oh no, is there something I can do?"

"No, sweetie, you've got your own messes to figure out."

"Tell me about it." Rochelle readjusted the candelabras.

"I wanted to call you because I know you need a friend right now, but I'm gonna go away for a little while."

"Where are you going?"

"Savannah…to see my daddy."

"That'll be good for you, but what about Barrington?"

"He's a big boy. He'll be out on bond soon, and the attorney Harry recommended is already workin' on Barrington's plea. But Barrington is a big boy, he made this mess all by himself, and he's gonna need to figure this one out on his own. Bless his heart."

Rochelle chuckled at the Southern phrase, something she learned when she first moved to Texas, didn't really mean what it sounded like. "Bless his heart, Maeve."

Maeve laughed, "Bless his heart." They both laughed together, a real laugh for Rochelle, for the first time in a long time. "I was thinkin', you can always come out to visit me and Daddy, if you need to get away. Barrington and I bought him a pretty old home with a big front porch. We can sit on the rockin' chairs and drink lemonade and just relax."

"That sounds wonderful, I'll think about it, thanks Maeve." Rochelle clicked her tongue and Moosh popped up in response, following her into the kitchen. All the Italian Marble was gone, along with the thin brown grout lines, only the subfloor remained.

"I feel bad about the other night, honeybee…about Harry's ashes and all. Barrington should have never put his paws on that urn."

"Yeah, that was a disaster. It's all cleaned up now." Rochelle threw the spent Q-tips into the trash can.

"I'm so sorry about Harry's affair," Maeve was aghast, "and with Christopher?"

"Oh, Maeve, what a mess…if you only knew."

"Do you think you and Christopher will be able to talk it out? Be able to be friends again?"

"You know, I was just thinking about that a minute ago, and well, we'll at least have a conversation."

"Good, he's gonna be lost without Mirabelle, you know. She and the girls left for China today."

"I'm beginning to think we're all lost, Maeve." Rochelle opened the door to the back yard, letting Moosh out. She kicked her shoes off, following behind him. "Have a safe trip."

"Love you, honeybee."

"Love you, too."

Rochelle stepped onto the plush grass, feeling the energy of the good earth beneath the soles of her feet, as she walked over to her makeshift nest. It had been few days since she'd checked on the fledgling. Peeking in, she saw the nest was empty. *Good.* Baby was finally strong enough to leave the nest and fly with Mama. *Good for you, Mama, enjoy your baby.*

Rochelle's phone rang, it was Detective Blankenship. "Hello, Detective."

"Mrs. Hawthorne, there's been a break in the case."

With phone to ear, Rochelle clicked her tongue again as she made her way back into the house, her dog-baby following behind.

47

PERSPECTIVE

W hat the fuck just happened, and who the fuck *was* that? That was *not* the Christopher I loved. No, *that* Christopher was gone—both literally and figuratively, altered by drugs and drink, and God knows what else. *That,* was a monstrous incarnation of himself. What did he just do? Stab me and leave me to die?

I lay immobile, watching Moosh gobble the scrambled eggs from the broken plate on the kitchen floor, wolfing in every last bit, including my ring. Unbelievable! He trotted over to me as I lay there, giving my forehead a sniff and a lick, before exiting through the doggy door. My outsides were paralyzed, my insides felt nauseous and anxious, watching the tiny red footprints Moosh left behind as he walked away.

I was dying. Wheezing as I was bleeding out, unable to move, unable to speak, unable to swallow nor eject the object stuck in my throat. Red blood stained white marble as the scene turned black.

∾

WEARY BODY, a lump on the floor, Christopher pushed himself up to standing, and switched off the vacuum cleaner, gulping in air as his sobs turned to hiccups. He picked up the knife, discolored with Harry's dried blood and held it to his own neck, as his throat convulsed with spasms, pressing the blade—pressing, drawing a thin line of blood, but nothing more. He threw the knife to the floor, unable to go through with it, unable to take his own life. He was a coward.

What was he to do now? Christopher paced as he frantically dialed Mirabelle's cell, the call went directly to voicemail. Christopher knew she was on a flight to China, but he dialed again anyway, wanting to hear her recorded message, needing her voice to calm him. Tears poured from his swollen eyes, as he curled into a ball on his sofa, staring at the pile of filthy clothes, and the knife, wondering what he was going to do.

I FELT the bright beam of light warming my closed eyelids. Was I dead? Nudged awake, I forced my eyes open with all my might, squinting as sunlight radiated through the doggy door. I watched, paralyzed, my breathing constricted and shallow, as Moosh popped his body through the small opening and scurried into the foyer.

Someone was at the door! I could hear her muffled voice, "Coming, Moosh! Mommy's home!" It was Rochelle! *Thank God!* I knew she'd be in the kitchen in no time…until I heard her say, "Oh my God! Moosh! What happened?" *In here, Rochelle! This happened!* It sounded like something fell to the floor, items rolled. *I'm in here!* I heard a shuffle and then nothing. Rochelle was gone.

CHRISTOPHER JUMPED FROM THE SOFA, still in his lounge clothes, and traded his house shoes for tennis shoes, tightening the laces. He grabbed the knife and the pile of clothing, wrapping the jacket around the knife and shoving it all into a green garbage bag. He pulled on a ball cap and grabbed his car keys, opening the front door only to see Detective Blankenship standing there.

"Christopher Campbell?"

"Yes?"

"Are you going somewhere?"

"I was, uh...just taking out the trash." Christopher held the bag, containing the clothing and knife. He looked down at the additional garbage bag, filled with empty bottles, that he'd put out earlier.

"Mr. Campbell, I'm going to need you to come with me, to answer a few questions about your friend Harry Hawthorne."

"OK."

"You can go ahead and leave your garbage bag with the other one, and tend to that later."

Christopher clutched the bag to his chest, looking down at Harry's ring, a bit too large for his finger. "No, I think we should bring this with us."

I WAS BARELY THERE, confused, and lightheaded. Was I even breathing? My heart rate was quick and weak. Was I hallucinating? I thought I heard Rochelle's voice again, talking to Moosh. "OK, have it your way." *Please, Rochelle...over here.* It took all of my remaining strength to will my eyes open. I heard her, she was on the other side of the island. I heard water running. I knew she couldn't see me. I was screaming inside, but unable to call out for help. *Just a few more feet!*

My paralyzed body was hidden from view but a river of my blood escaped, trailing all the way to the end of the island. If she would just look down. I heard Rochelle's footsteps getting closer, nearing the end of the red river, footsteps, then silence. Silence, until Rochelle screamed.

48

THE SHOVEL

"I appreciate your business Mrs. Hawthorne."

Rochelle signed the paperwork and handed the man a check. "No…thank *you!* I'm going to love my new floor. Thank you for getting it done so quickly."

"Yes, ma'am, I appreciate ya payin' double to have two teams come do the work. That was our quickest job ever. Call us if you'll be needin' anything else."

"Will do." Rochelle closed the front door and made her way into the kitchen, Moosh following closely behind. Rochelle loved the fresh, slightly musky smell of the new hardwood and the way it looked. She especially loved the way it added a warmth to her kitchen, a warmth that had never been there before. Apparently Moosh also like the smell of hardwood as he happily sniffed the hand-scraped planks. "What do you smell baby? Do you like your new floor?" Rochelle placed OH SHIT under the spout of the Bosch coffee maker and pressed the button to grind the beans. Turning to watch Moosh as he sniffed and sniffed. "Come over here, baby."

Moosh didn't listen. He kept his nose to the floor, sniffing the same place—the place once inhabited by the thin brown grout lines. *Oh no!* The coffee started to trickle into the mug as Rochelle called to her dog.

"Moosh, baby, come here!" Moosh didn't listen. Instead, he started to scratch the floor with his front paw, alternating sniffing and scratching. Rochelle grew anxious, watching her little dog scratch the same place, the place she found Harry.

Rochelle neared her naughty puppy, scooping him up into her arms. "You listen to Mommy, young man!" she reprimanded as she peered down to the place on the floor that grabbed his attention. Moosh licked Rochelle's face and she tickled under his chin as she quietly scanned the graining of the wood with her eyes, scanning for thin brown grout lines. She slowly bent down, peering closer, closer, when a loud bang and a knock on the door startled her. *Jesus!* Her coffee maker hissed, signaling it was finished.

Rochelle approached the door with Moosh in her arms, he yipped as she pulled the door open, revealing to her a small, beige man, with coke-bottle glasses, wearing an orange vest and holding a shovel. "Earl?"

"Well, lookie here!" Earl seemed pleased with himself. "I cain't hardly believe my eyes! I been lookin' fer ya since ya skedaddled out the garden center!"

The backfire of the old, beat-up Ford truck idling in her driveway caused Rochelle to jump and Moosh to yip again. The old woman in the driver's seat smiled a toothless grin and shrugged her shoulders as Rochelle raised a hand to her chest. Earl started to laugh, then cough, uncontrollably, leaning on the shovel for support, his beige face turning fuchsia as he tried to catch his breath.

Moosh barked as Earl coughed, and Rochelle shushed her little dog. Earl regained his composure. "I'm sorry little lady! That there's Bessie."

"Oh," Rochelle gave a slight wave to the toothless woman, whose mouth hung open, scanning Rochelle's mansion from behind the wheel. "Is that your wife?"

"Who?"

"Bessie?"

Earl laughed again, controlling himself this time, so as not to erupt into another coughing jag. "No...that's not my wife! I remember, you sure were funny, little lady. Bessie is my truck!"

"Oh," Rochelle blushed.

"That there beaut' behind the wheel...that there's Mabel...my girlfriend."

"Oh," Rochelle giggled.

"Anyways, it's not too often we drive up to the big city, but I got me a pig and a package I gotta pick up in McKinney. Seems someone got to thinkin' it was a good idea to buy a pig as a birthday present for a seven-year-old. I mean, they are kinda cute and all, when they're little pink piglets, but folks don't get to thinkin' 'bout just how big pigs're gonna be when they're all growed up! That there pig is gonna grow to be about five hunnerd pounds or more! Them there folks cain't take care of her the right way no more."

"Well that's fascinating, Earl, and kind of you. So you're adopting the pig? As a pet? Do you have a farm?"

"Yeah, we got some land, some chickens, an' a swayback horse."

"No pigs?"

"Well...not any more...we done ate all of 'em."

Rochelle clutched Moosh to her chest. "Oh...right...how can I help you, Earl?"

"Well, seems like I got to thinkin' about that darned pig, excuse my language, and then started thinkin' about all the things they're good for. Besides eatin', I mean. Like, makin' clothin' outa them, or brushes...and they're good smellers ya know! Did y'all know that? Some pigs can smell out fancy mushrooms—the kind fancy people eat! You prob'ly know that, on a count'a yer fancy. Anyways...another thing they're good for is eatin' people! Like when someone wants to get rid of a body, they chop that dang thing up, and feed it to them there pigs. So, that got me thinkin' 'bout you!"

Rochelle slammed the door as Earl continued to talk through the crack. "Now wait a darn minute, excuse my language, don't go gittin' yer feelin's hurt. I didn't mean it in any other way but, I got to thinkin' about ya and wanted ta git ya yer shovel. I mean, ya done paid for it and all...that's all...plain an' simple. I know you weren't goin' to be hidin' no body, no matter what Liberty said. I can tell, yer a reg'lar ol' ama-teur. So I'm gonna leave this here shovel on yer fancy porch for ya, on a count'a ya paid for it an' all. That's it! Don't be gettin' all in a huffy." Earl spoke to himself as he propped the shovel against the house and descended the stairs, mumbling. "City folk—always gettin' their britches in a twist. MABEL...LET'S GIT TO GITTIN'!"

Earl opened the creaking door to the truck and hopped in, waving out the window as Mabel backed out of the driveway, Earl calling out, "Have yerself a blessed day!" The truck backfired one more time as it slowly chugged off.

49

VISITING CHRISTOPHER

C hristopher looked smaller to Rochelle—shrunken, a Claymation form of himself, as he sat in an orange plastic chair on the other side of the penitentiary glass. No longer a unique trendsetter in a curated wardrobe, Christopher drowned in a nondescript prison uniform, looking like any other inmate. Like the ones Rochelle watched being interviewed on *Dateline*. Christopher picked up the receiver in the booth to speak, Rochelle did the same.

"Hi," she said, searching his defeated face for any former version of himself.

"Hi..." His darkened eyes dropped, "thank you for coming to see me."

"Of course..."

Christopher nervously pulled at the stitching on his loose V-neck, his own neck looked rail thin.

"We're still friends, Christopher."

Tears flooded Christopher's eyes as he choked back sobs, unable to speak. Rochelle waited patiently for him to regain his composure. "How, Rochelle? How can you forgive me for what I've done?"

"I can forgive you, because you didn't *mean* to hurt Harry."

"I didn't, *my God* I didn't."

"You were out of your mind on drugs, Christopher...it wasn't you."

"It wasn't...but it *was* me," Christopher hands shook as he pushed his glasses up the bridge of his nose. The frames appeared too big for his wan face.

"It was a crime of passion, Christopher. Isn't that what they call it? Unplanned...unintended," Rochelle wondered if Christopher's dreams haunted him at night, if Harry's dying face kept him awake, if he ever randomly felt Harry's touch on his shoulder.

"I didn't mean to..."

"I know." Rochelle took a deep breath and blew it out, sitting up a little bit straighter. "I'm going to ask the court to be lenient on you."

"You are?"

"Yes, I don't even know if it will help any. But I'm going to try."

"Oh, thank God!" Christopher nervously looked around at the other inmates talking to their visitors, avoiding eye contact with them. He seemed paranoid as he leaned in closer to the glass, covering his mouth and whispering into the receiver, "It's *awful* in here! I'm *so afraid*."

"I can't imagine." The artificial scent of the tropical room deodorizer, automatically spraying at timed intervals, could not cover the underlying stench of ancient sewer. Rochelle knew she was going to have to wash her clothing when she got home.

"Why would you do this for me, Rochelle?"

"Because, I understand. I understand the frustration, the helplessness...the betrayal. I understand what would drive somebody...you...to go temporarily insane."

"You do?"

"Yes! You *were* having an affair with my husband! But when I think about it, I can't be mad at Harry for being gay...or fluid...or whatever he was. But I *can* be *irate* that he took away my chance of having children with him. Eight years...it was eight years of lies."

"But, you told him you were pregnant. You told all of us."

"I know, I did. I was angry."

"But...you didn't know about the affair?"

"I didn't."

"Why then, why were you angry?"

"Harry had a vasectomy, Christopher, a secret vasectomy, eight years ago...without telling me." Rochelle's eyes became misty. "I wanted to make him sweat a bit, teach him a lesson."

"But...but..."

"He needed to squirm a little for what he'd hidden from me."

"Teach him a lesson?" Christopher's eyes turned stormy, "This was all over a lie?"

Rochelle could see the wheels in Christopher's mind start turning, recalling her lie, the lie that started it all, the lie that sent Christopher on a bender, putting him so out of his mind, so far out of his mind, he stabbed the only man he ever loved. She could see him recalling his actions, emotions playing out on his face, knuckles turning white as he gripped the receiver, chest heaving with rapid breath.

"This is your fault!"

"What?" Rochelle was confused. "No."

Christopher dropped the phone receiver, and slammed both hands on the glass in front of Rochelle's face. Rochelle jumped out of her chair. The guard behind Christopher lunged forward and grabbed him by the arms, pulling Christopher back, away from the glass.

"This is *your* fault!" Christopher screamed and fought, letting his body weight fall, as the guard dragged him backward. "If you didn't lie, Harry wouldn't be dead! I wouldn't be in this filthy hell hole!" The guard pulled Christopher, feet spragging, through the door. He disappeared, screaming, "This is your fault, you bitch!"

Rochelle stood, cold with adrenaline, body trembling, as both phone receivers swung in place on either side of the glass. *What just happened?* The other inmates and their visitors stared at her, as she remained frozen, feeling herself shrink in the bleak gray room. Rochelle jumped when a guard touched her arm.

"I'm sorry, ma'am. I didn't mean to scare you, are you OK?"

"Yes," Rochelle smoothed her frazzled hair away from her face, "I'm fine, thank you...just a little shaken."

"He won't be allowed back. Can I escort you out?"

"Yes, yes, thank you."

ROCHELLE STOOD at the front window signing herself out of the visitor's area. The smell of burnt coffee clung to her nostrils as she waited for her belongings to be returned to her. The outside door opened, and in walked Detective Blankenship with another man, backlit by the beginnings of a pink sunset.

"Mrs. Hawthorne, I heard you were here."

"Hi, Detective. I came to check on Christopher."

"Well, that's mighty big of you."

Rochelle smiled flatly.

"Here you go, ma'am." The female officer from behind the glass held Rochelle's purse out the window.

"Oh, thank you." Rochelle took her purse and slid the straps up her shoulder.

"Mrs. Hawthorne, this is Detective Sean McGovern, he's visiting from up north."

Detective McGovern held out his hand, "Ma'am."

"Seems the Yankees want to see how we Southern boys do things," Detective Blankenship winked at her.

"Hi, Detective," Rochelle shook Detective McGovern's firm, warm grip. His kind eyes were soft green moss, but his gaze was intense. She felt flush. Electric. "Well, it was nice meeting you." Rochelle let go and pulled a fallen purse strap up her shoulder.

"Mrs. Hawthorne, this is for you." Detective Blankenship held out a small manila envelope.

"What's this?" Rochelle took the envelope from the detective, lifted the flap, and peeked inside, where she saw two bands, nestled close to each other—two lovers, taunting her.

"Those're the two rings...you know...from the case. Seems like you're the one who should have them. Your husband buying them, and all."

"Ah, yes, thank you." Rochelle could feel Detective McGovern watching her, she straightened her shoulders as Detective Blankenship continued.

"I heard you might talk to the courts, ask them to be lenient on your friend, Mr. Campbell."

"I've changed my mind," Rochelle raised her head in confidence. "He stabbed my husband, he just tried to attack me, I wouldn't feel safe with him out, walking the streets."

"Well, that's understandable, ma'am."

Rochelle looked down at the envelope in her hand, "Thank you for these, I've got to get home and let Moosh out."

"Yes, ma'am, don't let us keep you," the detective tipped his hat. "How's that little one doing, anyway?"

"He's just great!" Rochelle couldn't leave quickly enough—she just wanted to get home to Moosh.

∽

THE DETECTIVES WATCHED Rochelle hurriedly exit the building and proceeded to sign themselves in at the front desk.

"Pretty lady," Detective McGovern showed his credentials to the officer behind the glass.

"Yep," Detective Blankenship chuckled, scribbling his signature "She won't be back here."

"Was she visiting her husband?"

"No way, he was the vic. Her husband was having an affair. He was stabbed to death by his lover. *That's* who she was visiting."

"Visiting the other woman? Is this a coed pen?"

"No," Detective Blankenship belly laughed, "she was visiting the other *man*."

Detective McGovern blushed, "Oh, I see."

"For a minute, we thought she was the perp...but she checked out. Sally, buzz us in." The officer behind the desk hit the buzzer and Detective Blankenship opened the door, holding it for Detective McGovern.

"Thanks," Detective McGovern walked through, "glad you got your man. I just don't think *she's* as innocent as she seems."

"Huh," Detective Blankenship let the door swing, "you don't say?" The lock clamped shut.

It was an unusually cool summer day as Rochelle descended the steps of the penitentiary, happy to leave the drab, gray setting behind, while moving forward toward the pink Texas skyline. She hopped into Harry's Jaguar and placed her purse on the passenger seat. She clipped her seatbelt, pushed the ignition button, and listened to the car purr itself awake. She pressed another button on the dash, and the convertible top slowly opened, revealing to her a lovely, endless watercolor sky, before tucking itself into its compartment. She slid a scarf out from her purse, inadvertently pulling out the small manila envelope with it, as it fell into the passenger seat. She tied back her long hair with the scarf and lifted the envelope from the seat. Opening it, she let the two bands fall out and onto her palm. She placed the envelope aside and collected both rings, sliding the smooth metal bands onto her pointer finger. She gripped the top of the steering wheel with both hands, the handsome rings in her line of sight.

Rochelle placed the car in drive and slowly stepped on the gas, making her way out of the parking lot. She adjusted her rearview mirror, watching the visitors' section of the penitentiary disappear in the background.

Thump! Something hit her windshield. It was a bird! *Flutter-flutter, tip-tap.* Rochelle slammed on the brakes, her heart pounding. The bird fluttered off the hood of the car and onto the ground, desperately flapping its disabled wings, trying to take flight. Rochelle watched in horror as the injured bird writhed on the ground, wounded and helpless.

50

A NEW PERSPECTIVE

I watched through blurred vision as Rochelle screamed, frightened by the grotesque sight of me, of me—half dead, lying in a pool of my own blood, as it pulsed from my body and seeped deep into the grout between the white marble slabs. Even Moosh didn't dare come near me.

It couldn't have been easy for Rochelle—seeing me that way. I knew she loved me. It must have been horrifying, her having to find me in that state. I didn't want her to worry, I really couldn't feel a thing. Funny, when death is upon you, how calm you become. I was strangely peaceful, although I could feel my heart flutter inside my chest, desperately trying to regain its rhythm. Without blood, how could it? My heart haplessly pattered, trying its best to keep me alive. Maybe it was trying to keep itself alive. Maybe I was just the vessel and my heart was the being. It's funny how philosophical one gets when they are dying. Fuck.

At least Rochelle was there, at least she found me. I had a chance. Rochelle would save me.

~

ROCHELLE SCREAMED, scaring Moosh, who opted to take comfort under the dining room table. The sight of Harry lying there, bleeding out, was horrifying. Rochelle panicked, covering her eyes, afraid to look. She found her purse and fumbled through, searching for her phone, she needed to call someone, send for help, she pressed nine, one—then stopped. She stared at her keypad, one more number would summon help for her lying, er, dying husband. Rochelle turned her head to look at Harry, sprawled on the floor, motionless, helpless. Helpless like a wounded bird. *Flutter-flutter tip-tap.* She tiptoed closer, trying not to step on the river of sticky blood, and leaned forward, her face close to his. Yes, he was alive, he was barely there, but he was there—unable to move, unable to speak, his panicked eyes the only way to communicate with her.

Her tears fell onto his face as she leaned over him, asking, "Harry? Can you hear me?"

Harry moved his eyeballs ever so slightly.

He can! Rochelle let out the breath she didn't know she was holding. "Good!"

Still clutching her phone, Rochelle turned to look behind her, toward the kitchen table and the six chairs gathered around it. She wondered why they bothered buying six chairs, she and Harry, when there would only ever be two of them eating family dinners together. Why would Harry bother agreeing to such a purchase when he knew their family wasn't going to expand? Rochelle walked over to the table and placed her phone on top, dragging one of the chairs nearer to Harry, setting it down, avoiding any of his messy blood. Rochelle sat in the chair and leaned forward.

"You've made such a mess, Harry." She wiped her tears on her sleeve, assessing the red river. "*This* is going to be so hard to clean up. But, you're not going to be here to bitch about it, are you?"

Harry's panicked eyeballs moved rapidly.

"I can't imagine who did this to you, but I'm sure they had a good reason."

Harry's eyes questioned her as a tear fell backward from his eye, collecting in his ear.

"What's that? You don't think someone would have a reason to do this to you? Good old Harry, good old *hard working*, always doing the *right thing*, *Honest Harry*? Ha!" Rochelle shook her finger at Harry, "No...someone *definitely* had a reason to do this to you!" There was horror on her face but strength in her words, as her tears flowed, "What did you do to *them*? How did you make them suffer, *Honest Harry*? It doesn't matter. *YOU*, are a lie, your life is a lie, *our* life is a lie." Rochelle broke down, barely eking out, "Our *future children* are a lie!" Rochelle took a moment to collect herself. "All that bullshit about our dreams. Our aspirations? Where did all that go? Hmm?" Rochelle waited for an answer she knew wasn't coming.

"Let me help you here, and I'll be quick, because I see you're running out of time. I found the *real* Harry...no, I *discovered* the real Harry. The lying, cheating, heartless Harry! Do you *know* where he was? He was hidden behind a code *CPT-55250*. Do you know what that means? Sure you do. You signed the fucking paper! The real Harry was scribbled on a fucking pink paper, and cowardly stuffed into the lining of a briefcase. You've got to be kidding me! Eight years, Harry! Eight years you hid a fucking vasectomy from me? Telling *ME,* I'm the one who was broken? All those years...all those years I cried to you, sobbed on your shoulders, barely able to breathe, barely able to take another step forward, and you AGREED WITH ME THAT I WAS THE ONE WHO WAS BROKEN?" Spittle flew from her mouth onto Harry's face as she spoke, the light quickly fading in his eyes. Rochelle's mouth quivered. "All those years...all those years I put you first, Harry. All those years I chose YOU. Well, today...I choose me."

Rochelle waited for Harry's last breath before she dialed 911.

FIN.

EARL

Elsewhere...

Tires crunched and popped along stones and branches as Earl and Mabel pulled onto the dusty drive leading up to their small farmhouse.

"Nice fella, wadn't he?" Earl bounced in his seat as they made their way up the bumpy drive.

"Yup, that he was," Mabel kept her eyes on the road.

Two wooden rocking chairs sat on a peeling white porch as clothing on a nearby line blew in the warm, country breeze.

"Gave us a real good deal, didn't he?"

"Yup, that he did." Mabel stepped on the gas to encourage the truck's trek up the slight embankment toward the dilapidated barn, causing the truck to backfire, startling the pig in the crate in the bed of the truck.

"Now, take it easy there, Mabel. We don't want to go scarin' the life outta that there pig already." Earl pushed his heavy glasses up his nose as he turned and squinted out the truck's smudged back window, checking on their cargo.

"Now, I ain't gonna do nothin' like that, Earl."

"Well, I'm just sayin', ain't every day we git to git a free pig."

"Amen to that."

Mabel pulled the truck behind the barn. The structure's faded red paint gave it an eerie appearance as the sun hung low behind it. Vines, old and new, clung and rose along the weathered boards, intertwining themselves all the way up to the cupola, the last strand of vegetation choking the rusted weathervane.

"Pull 'er right over there." Earl pointed to the pen behind the barn where a few chickens fought with a rooster. An old mare looked on, lazily swatting flies from herself with her tail. "Now, back 'er in nice and easy."

"Yup," Mabel backed the truck up to the gate as Earl guided her, his head popped out of the passenger side window.

"Easy...easy...right there!" Earl instructed as Mabel stepped on the squeaky brake. Earl complimented her parking. "Dang, Mabel, yer a reg'lar ol' val-*LET*. Let's get this cargo unloaded."

"Yup."

Both Mabel and Earl opened their creaking doors, each meandering their way out of the truck and onto the dusty earth. Earl pulled the rusty tailgate down while Mabel fetched a step stool and climbed up and into the truck bed, being careful not to step on the large, mounded plastic tarp lying next to the pig crate.

"Ya ready, Earl?"

"Now hang on a darn toot, Mabel." Earl struggled to jostle a ramp onto the back of the truck and then reached to open the gate of the pen enclosure behind him. He pushed his glasses up his nose and wiped the perspiration from his forehead before saying, "OK, I'm a-waitin' fer ya."

Mabel unlatched the door of the pig crate and swung it open. "Now come on, git!" She ordered the pig, but the pig just stood there, looking at Mabel. "Now come on," she waved her hand to usher it out, "git!" The pig was not having it.

"Well...I see we're off like a herd a turtles...what in the sam-hell are ya waitin' for?"

"Earl, save that sass for someone else, dang swine won't budge."

"Well, quit yer piddling' and slap 'er on the ass!"

Mabel reached into the crate and gave the pig a swat, which sent the swine squealing as it barreled down the ramp and into the pen. Earl shut the gate behind it, clapping dust away from his hands.

"Ha!" Earl wheezed. "Dang swine made such a ruckus, she gon' wake the possums!"

"We gotta git 'er fed, Earl," Mabel called from the truck. "Come help me with this tarp."

"Alrighty, can ya push from the back, while I pull?"

"Yup," Mabel walked behind the mounded tarp. "Ya ready?"

"Yessum."

Mabel squatted in her floral country shift, letting out a little gas as she did. "Scuse me."

"What?" Earl squinted at Mabel through his thick lenses.

"Never you mind. Ya ready?"

"Now, dang it, woman. I already said I was ready."

Mabel pushed her end of the tarp with a grunt as Earl pulled on his. Sliding the wrapped mass down the ramp and onto the ground.

"Now, come on down here, Mabel. You do the choppin' an' I'll empty the wheelbarrah."

Earl offered his hand to Mabel, helping her out of the truck bed. He whistled as he strolled over to a large and rusty wheelbarrow covered with a similar tarp. Earl pushed his glasses up the bridge of his nose before grabbing the handles of the wheelbarrow, lifting it, and pushing it away from the barn, whistling as he walked toward a small clearing in between the trees.

A creek babbled in the distance as Earl walked between the trees, toward a patch of earth, where a shovel with a pointed tip was stuck into the ground. A flock of grackles puttered around a large hole dug into the mossy earth, until Earl yelled, "Git!" They all fluttered to the treetops, looking down with tilted heads, watching the small beige man as he worked.

Earl pushed his wheelbarrow to the edge of the cavernous hole and removed the tarp, revealing large bones—human bones, ones that were too big for his previous pigs to devour. Earl grabbed the handles of the wheelbarrow and raised it, sending skulls and fractured femurs into the hole, toppling them onto others, half hidden in dirt, having been dumped there before.

Earl pulled the shovel out of the ground and started to push dirt into the hole to cover the bones as he whistled. The sound of a chainsaw whirred in the distance.

ACKNOWLEDGMENTS

THANK YOU, for taking the time to read Dinner With The Hawthornes—my second published attempt at word assemblage, as I continue to try to create unique and interesting stories. I am truly grateful beyond words.

I've said it before, without readers, our books would be orphans, our stories would go unread and our imaginations would grow stagnant. You are the reason we strive to be good at what we do.

Also, thank you so much to all who have helped me along the way:

Officer Maureen (Mo) Messner, for your consult, and most of all for your choice to protect and serve.

Tex Thompson, for, once again sharing your unending wealth of developmental wisdom and for continually reminding me to add more unfortunate adventure.

My critique sisters, Jane and Janet, for reading each week and sharing your eyes, edits and ideas, you make me a better writer. Thank you both for your support. It's so much fun to be in your tribe.

My alpha readers:

Maureen Davis—friend, amazing writer and well-read eye.

Roy Alexander, for being one of my biggest cheerleaders, relentlessly messaging on Facebook, "When will book two be out?"

My mom, Margie, thanks for instilling a hard work ethic and unending creativity in me. The apple doesn't fall far from the tree.

To my creative kids (see...apples, tree), Roman and Marcella for patiently listening on the other end of the line every time I called, even when I read you chapters you'd already heard. I respect your perspectives and am forever proud of you... xx

Lastly, thank you to Earl, my appliance guy...and friend. For coming to my house every week to buy copies of The Suicide of Sophie Rae to pass them out to your friends, neighbors and clients. Your support means so much...and, I'm so happy my appliances work!

∽

ABOUT THE AUTHOR

CHERIE FRUEHAN is an artist and author who was born and raised in Scranton, Pennsylvania. She earned her BFA from Marywood, University and credits her education as inspiring her to dabble in all things creative. She now resides in Dallas, Texas with her husband and two dogs. A member of MENSA, her artwork has been featured on the front cover and inside pages of MENSA magazine.

www.cheriefruehan.com

ALSO BY CHERIE FRUEHAN

The Suicide of Sophie Rae

Made in the USA
Coppell, TX
25 February 2020